I0778851

LEGEND OF THE Time Witches

THE NEXT GENERATION

SR Sutton

Copyright @2023 by Stephen Robert Sutton

All rights reserved. No part of this book may be reproduced in any form or by any electronic or mechanical means, including information storage and retrieval systems, without permission in writing from the publisher, except by reviewers, who may quote brief passages in a review.

This publication contains the opinions and ideas of its author. It is intended to provide helpful and informative material on the subjects addressed in the publication. The author and publisher specifically disclaim all responsibility for any liability, loss or risk, personal or otherwise, which is incurred as a consequence, directly or indirectly, of the use and application of any of the contents of this book.

WORKBOOK PRESS LLC
187 E Warm Springs Rd,
Suite B285, Las Vegas, NV 89119, USA

Website: https://workbookpress.com/
Hotline: 1-888-818-4856
Email: admin@workbookpress.com

Ordering Information:
Quantity sales. Special discounts are available on quantity purchases by corporations, associations, and others.
For details, contact the publisher at the address above.

ISBN-13:   978-1-961845-69-5 (Paperback Version)
              978-1-961845-68-8 (Digital Version)

REV. DATE: 10/03/2023

LEGEND OF THE TIME WITCHES

THE NEXT GENERATION

S R SUTTON

LEGEND OF THE TIME WITCHES
THE NEXT GENERATION

The years moved on, and gradually the time witches Crystal, Natasha, Shanice and Elaina decided to go their own way. They stayed in contact with each other, but it was time to stand aside for a new generation of time witches. Shanice was the first to leave, she re-joined her family on earth and her dear friends Kayleigh and Jessica, and they went to university together. Natasha got married to Doran and they had two children together, they lived on a planet near Crystal. Elaina went to work at the federation base and joined, Angelica once more as a couple. Crystal looked after her father Zenith on their planet Aspera, joined by Strania and Shimick. They all had many adventures together fighting vampires, robots, space pirates and dark witches. But it was time to rest and let another generation of time witches to combat evil and save lives in time and space. Luna, Maya, Jessica and Alicia were the new generation of time witches.

LEGEND OF THE TIME WITCHES

THE NEXT GENERATION

S R SUTTON

LEGEND OF THE TIME WITCHES –NEXT GENERATION

INTRODUCTION

The Original time witches went their separate ways, leaving an opening for four more-time witches, namely Maya who was a relative of Shanice. Luna's friend of Maya's otherwise known as the moonchild, Alicia a friend from magic school and her sister Jessica. Each one of them had great powers as white witches, they had known the time witches, and wanted to continue their work. Like all white witches they considered life as precious and they were friends of the earth, with a desire to help and heal people. The new generation time witches visited their predecessors by going back in time when they were active, by this time they were in their twenties, helping them fight the evil Bula Seraph, who was spreading his Bula virus. It took both generations of witches to defeat him, but at what cost? And what did it mean for their future?

The enemies continued to torment them, from vampires, dark witches, androids, space pirates and other creatures, chasing them through time and space. Devil like demons called Lamians were also pursuing them, conjured up by Bula Seraph the evil wizard. Their ventures took them to many time periods, both in the past and future, meeting famous people and places. Their many powers proved useful such as Ergokensis, pyrokinesis, psychokinesis, levitation, clairvoyance, psychometry, telepathy and many more.

And so, the legend of the time witches, continues with the next generation, in previous stories you can read about their adventures, and then read this book. The books are designed to entertain you, educate you, and hopefully make you think of your planet, care for your environment, and protect the earth and its inhabitants.

Contents

ACKNOWLEDGMENTS

I wish to thank so many people who have supported me during the time I have been writing this book, I am so pleased with them all.

Thank you to the three people who have modelled for the time witches namely Natalie Sartora as Natasha, Shell Bridgart as Crystal, Shara Alexandra as Shanice all friends and colleagues from the midlands and Amy Wiener as Elaina (Amy is from New York).

Thank you to my Granddaughter Ella Jay Briggs for her input and support for her character Maya.

Thank to friends and family who believed in me and my pending success.

Thanks to my parents Rita and Len Sutton for their encouragement in my writing.

My legacy goes to my children Gemma, Jeni, Mike and Dan.

Thank you to Sandra Harker for helping to design the time witch's outfits.

Introducing Laura Dawn Standley modelling on the front cover for the character clairvoyant Laura Dawn. Not forgetting Tyeshia Sturgis as Angelica featured throughout the books as Elaina's girlfriend.

ABOUT THE AUTHOR

Stephen Robert Sutton author and poet has written many books, some in his own name others under other names such as Sarah Ruth Scott and Simon Robert Sinclair. The reason for more than one name was to write from a more feminine perspective drawing from his working colleagues and good female friends. The other was to write in various subjects providing knowledge from past experiences and studies of people. Some stories have been altered and include his real name for credibility; Stephen is also an artist and photographer who likes to work on most of his own book covers. When he wrote cracked porcelain it was it was based on factual events on psychiatric wards and experiences of nurses both on the wards and in the community. It is Stephen hope that one day he will see his work on Netflix and other movie companies that will portray his work as it is in his books. Stephen is dyslexic and dyspraxia and self-educated, he believes in self-motivation and the encouragement of others to enable him to keep writing, to date he has written.

https://stevesuttonsrsbooks.com/

https://stephensuttonbooks.com/

QUOTE

NATURE IS MY RELIGION, AND THE EARTH IS MY CHURCH

MAYA

Maya seemed a confident girl, she often led her friends in play and decided what they should all do for games. But below the surface of that girl was a world of uncertainty and a collection of phobias for her to deal with. She was small in stature and a little over weight, she had ginger hair and wore glasses, she loved trendy clothes and often voiced her opinion, which sometimes upset others. Maya loved art and design, she was very dramatic, often impersonating other people, especially teachers. But most of all she loved magic and watched programs containing magic and illusionists, she had her own magic set and practiced tricks on her friends. Maya also loved history and travelling to exciting places, exploring and capturing the atmosphere of historical places like Egypt and Rome.

One evening Maya had her own magic show, with a small audience consisting of her mother, father relatives and friends, it was all performed well, using music as an added bonus to the atmosphere. For an amateur performance it was a splendid show with a variety of tricks that Maya was able to convince people that magic did exist. But of course, it was all an illusion and not to be taken seriously. However, Natasha was put inside a box and she transformed herself into a cat for Maya. The two collaborated on this one and no one could explain how that was done, because it was really magic.

The next morning, Maya was eating her breakfast, when she managed to hear a conversation with her cousin Shanice and the time witches, they were discussing their adventures and just happened to mention Egypt and Cleopatra.

"You have been to Egypt?" she said, almost choking on her breakfast.

"Yes, back in time," Shanice said proudly.

"Back in history?" she said, puzzled.

"Time travelling," Crystal explained. "We went back to see Cleopatra."

"Yes, we transformed ourselves into cats," Shanice said, touching her face and purring.

"Awesome," Maya said.

"Now then," her mother said, enough of this nonsense.

"Maya, eat your breakfast or you will be late for school!"

Her mother Alison hated stories about witches, she was a very practical person who considered fairy tales as nonsense. She also questioned the credibility of her so-called family of witches, according to her they were just eccentric and possibly mentally unstable. She did like Shanice but she felt that she was away with the fairies and not in touch with reality almost like a moon child in another world, moon gazing. When the time witches returned, they all sat down for a while, and then Elaina went for a rest.

Foster was activated ready to navigate the ship into space, all the cabin doors locked as the ship was about to take off, Foster and Crystal checked the instruments and set the coordination's to travel to the space federation.

When they arrived at the federation base, Foster noticed a surge of energy and irregular readings on the equipment.

"Who is in the treatment room?" he asked.

"It might be Elaina," Crystal replied.

Elaina entered the room and sat beside Shanice, everybody looked at her strangely.

"Are you all right?" Natasha asked her.

"Yes, thank you," she replied. "Just need a rest in order to recharge my batteries."

"You have batteries?" Foster asked bewildered.

"It is a phrase, numpty," Shanice said, tutting. "A figment of speech."

"Where did you rest?" Crystal asked.

"In one of the cabins," Elaina replied, "Why?"

"Not in the treatment room?" Crystal enquired.

"What, no!" Elaina sharply replied.

"Are you sure?" Natasha asked.

"What is this, the Spanish inquisition?" Elaina shouted. "Of course not."

"Someone is in there," Foster said. "The equipment is still running."

"Shanice come with me," Natasha insisted. "We will investigate."

They looked in the treatment room and noticed Maya lying on the bed, she was fast asleep, and so they attempted to wake her, aware that she had been exposed to high levels of radiation. She eventually woke up feeling sick and disorientated, it had affected her badly, her vital body signs were out of control, showing many abnormalities. She was fighting for her life; her heart rate had increased with a high blood pressure. Natasha noticed that her heart had suddenly stopped beating and commenced cardiopulmonary resuscitation (CPR) She repeated the process until her heart started beating again and Maya began to respond by coughing with her eyes watering. She showed no signs at this point in gaining any powers, but that was normal as her body was seeking out her abilities by means of the radio activity within her. Shanice used a few spells to help stabilise her and allow her body to alter as it needed to with this new found energy. Gradually, as she was recovering, she began to levitate and then started moving objects with her mind, her arms were stretched out as objects began floating around the room. But she found it difficult controlling her powers and needed practice to refine it, this took weeks, but she was patient and guided by Shanice and Natasha.

Maya had followed Shanice aboard the ship and that was how she come to be there undetected, Foster had been deactivated for a while. Maya explained that wanted to know more about the time witches and so she wandered around looking everywhere around the ship, she eventually arrived in the treatment room. She noticed the instruments and began to examine them, and then tried out the bed, soon after she fell asleep. This set off the mechanism used to restore the powers to the time witches, she was being exposed to radiation omitted from the energy inside the meteor. She was unaware of the meteor or what the room was used for, she just thought it was a sleeping bay. Shanice seemed on edge, she was constantly acting strange and would not say why, just started pacing and muttering to herself.

"What's wrong Shan?" Natasha asked.

"Nothing really," she replied but continued pacing. This was usually an indication that Shanice was home sick, she missed her friends Kayleigh and Jessica and eventually did go home.

LUNA THE MOON CHILD

Once they were at the federation headquarters, the time witches went to see the commander and explained about the book of shadows and how it was sort after by so many people. Commander John Shepherd was discussing the problems affecting the galaxy such as the space pirates and the dark witches.

"Have you heard about a moon child?" Crystal asked.

"Yes, she is here in the base," he replied. "A bit strange, she lives in her own world, speaks nonsense."

"Can we see her?" she asked. "Maybe we can understand her."

"Be my guest," he said. "But all she speaks is gibberish."

"They say she sees visions like a prophet," Natasha said.

"Complete nonsense," he continued. "My men will lead you to her."

The guards led the time witches to the moon child, she was sat on the floor in a bright white room, with her legs crossed, dressed in a white outfit. She had blonde hair and looked about twelve years old, very much like Maya, but had a blank expression on her face. She lifted her arms and pulled a hut over her head when she noticed them near her, as if she was reluctant to speak to them. And then she began mumbling strange world, what she said was incomprehensible, as the commander said complete gibberish.

"Well, this is a waste of time, she is obviously gaga tapped," Shanice said.

"Don't be so judgemental Shan," Natasha said crossly.

"Well, look at her, do you think she is normal?" Elaina said, agreeing with Shanice.

"I understand her," Maya said, approaching the girl and smiling.

She spoke to the girl also talking strangely, and then the girl smiled and spoke again.

"Maya, you are so silly," Shanice began verbally attacking her.

"You are just making it up, to avoid getting in trouble."

"See the moon and cast a spell, in a while you will be well," Maya said, quoting the moon child.

And then to their astonishment the moon child produced an image of the book of shadows, everyone could see it, and then she continued to speak and Maya translated once again.

"The book of shadows tells the truth, what it says goes back to your youth."

"She is right. I read that in that room from the book," Shanice said.

"I have the proof; people of the moon know the truth," the moon child said.

"Moon child is a prophet," Maya said. "She is warning you of the dangers ahead."

Moon child had proven that she had the abilities to conjure up images and for see events in the future, she may have appeared odd but she had a special gift.

"What did she mean by casting a spell, and you would be well?" Crystal asked.

"She was referring to me gaining these powers, I must cast a moon spell to be well," Maya explained.

"Concentrate on your dream, listen to the voice and ignore the scream." The moon child said. "Luna is your friend at night, don't be seen in the light."

Maya smiled and the girl smiled back.

Maya introduced herself and moon child responded.

"She is called, Artemis or Luna, in Hebrew. Would you believe, Maya?" Mayer said.

"Well, you have turned out to be an asset, Maya," Natasha said.

"Wait," Maya said desperately. "Luna is telling me something."

"What is it?" Crystal asked.

"The man you are seeking has not got the book, but he is in danger on Delcara," Maya translated.

"The dead planet?" Crystal asked.

"Yes, where a virus killed many people," Maya explained.

"But we saw the book, he had it on the video," Natasha said.

"It could have got lost in the time portal," Shanice said.

"What else can she see?" Elaina asked.

Suddenly a vision appeared before them, it showed the moon and then the time portal. They saw Bula Seraph drifting down the time portal, and then he disappeared, he reappeared on Delcara and appeared unwell.

"The ghost came from that planet," Crystal said.

"Jay seemed to indicated that he was the only survivor," Natasha said.

"Yes, but was he?" Crystal said. "And virus could be still active in the environment."

"The Delcara virus was particularly nasty and spread like wild fire," Natasha said.

"But we discovered the antidote, which we left for the Earth people to inject themselves," Crystal said, proudly. "We saved millions of lives."

"We need to help Bula Seraph," Crystal said.

"One minute," Shanice interrupted. "Isn't he a wicked wizard?"

"Yes, and we are white witches," Crystal replied. "We save lives."

"We respect the life of others, no matter who they are" Natasha agreed.

"The point is do we take Luna with us" Crystal pondered.

"Let me ask her," Maya said, concerned.

"Isn't that risky?" Shanice said. "Taking miss moon struck."

"She will be useful," Elaina said.

"She is barking," Shanice said, unhappy with their decision.

"She agrees," Maya said. "As long as I can go."

"You will all have to be immunised," Natasha insisted, including the moon child."

"I think you are all mad," Shanice protested.

"You can always stay here Shan."

Shanice thought for a moment looking at Luna with a strange look on her face, she felt very uncomfortable in her presence.

"I will go and take care of Maya" she agreed.

The time witches returned to the commander with Luna following behind, they explained exactly what they had planned. The commander seemed reluctant at first, but then he knew the risks and how they could ensure the virus would be destroyed preventing the risk of it spreading across the universe. He finally agreed and told them to stay safe, he was still unsure about the moon child, but thought they could control her madness. At least Maya seemed to understand and support her, Maya also needed help developing her powers.

Alicia and Jessica

The sisters Alicia and Jessica Faber had grown up in a magical setting, with their parents Wizard Joseph and witch Marian Faber, as well as cousin Elaina. As children they had heard about the time witches, the legend of their adventures was often mentioned at magic school when they attended later. Two girls attended the school, that had been on some of the adventures, were Maya and Luna, they were unusual, even as far as witches go, Maya who was related to Shanice, was a ginger haired, bright eyed dreamer and Luna was the moonchild, quiet and a little weird who spoke in riddles. Both girls were picked on by others, targets for bullies and ridiculed for being different, but they didn't mind being different or odd. It was a big school for girls dedicated to the magical world, much like the boy's school, not far away. But of course, the school of magic didn't just have wizards and witches, but many other magical creatures and gifted aliens, those with extraordinary abilities that could be nurtured. The object of the schools was to bring out their talents and help them to use them to the best of their ability. Alicia and Jessica were slim girls looking alike apart from Alicia with her mousy hair and Jessica with darker hair. Both had hazel eyes and sunny smiles, apart from this their personalities and style of dress was different. Jessica professed to believe in self-preservation, while Alicia was very protective over others, rescuing stray pets.

A lot of people were curious of people with strange powers or the strange phenomenon such as the time witches displayed, this gave people around the universe a chance on discovering their powers. The school of magic opened up a program that catered for such people, aliens from distant planets attended, perfecting their skills. Extra sensory perception (E.S.P) was found in many human forms, this ability could be an ability in many forms and strengths said to derive from many energy sources. On earth it was found in meteors in Scotland, which came from the collision of two planets, which exploded and debris struck the earth, in the form of meteors containing radiation. The cave dwellers affected by this became powerful and divided into two groups the dark witches, serving evil and the white witches working for good.

- Clairvoyance — The ability to see things and events that are happening far away, and locate objects, places, people, using a sixth sense.

- Divination – The ability to gain insight into a situation using occult lists.

- Dowsing – The ability to locate water, sometimes using a tool called a dowsing rod.

- Dream telepathy- The ability to telepathically communicate with another person through dreams.

- Dermo-optical perception - The ability to perceive unusual sensory stimuli through one's own skin.

- Psychometry – The ability to obtain information about a person or an object by touch.[12]
- Precognition (including psychic premonitions) – The ability to perceive or gain knowledge about future events, without using induction or deduction from known facts.
- Remote viewing, telaesthesia or remote sensing – The ability to see a distant or unseen target using extrasensory perception.[14]
- Retrocognition or postcognition – The ability to supernaturally perceive past events.
- Telepathy – The ability to transmit or receive thoughts supernaturally.

These are a few abilities that people possess, some people are sceptical about such abilities particularly in the scientific world, years ago people would be hung or burned for having such gifts, even in the space age it is questioned. But the universe is a big place with wonders that are far beyond our comprehension, nothing is impossible. Beyond this universe is much more, and it is very distant more universes and many more places to explore in time.

One interesting fact of time travel was, being able to meet influential people in history such as Henry V111, Elizabeth 1, Cleopatra, Joan of Arc, Blackbeard and many more. School days became interesting when Alisia and Jessica arrived, the sisters got to know Maya and Luna almost immediately. Luna and Maya were being bullied by some of the older girls, and so Alicia and Jessica stepped in, using magic to combat them.

It was a bright sunny morning in September that Alisia and Jessica left New York on a shuttle to space, their destination was the school of magic on the planet Palletania, near the planet Rahattelon, where the space headquarters were located. Palletania was the rainbow planet, known for its colourful atmosphere that glowed like the morning sun. It looked magical, which is why the wizards and witches chose it, for the ideal location to build the magic schools. They used two very different designs for each school, a palace type building, taken from fairy tales for the girls, and a more modern design for the boys. Both buildings seemed to suit the landscape. They were the classical and the futuristic in a fusion of houses that surrounded them, of all colours, showing that time does not stand still, it moves on a perpetual cog in a clock in constant motion. Alicia and Jessica had entered a time portal, in the shuttle to reach Palletania in the future, as their ancestors did long ago. This was shortly after the cave dwellers of Alba/Scotland did during the battle of the witches, White witches fought to protect their good name, while the dark witches fought for evil, and their own greed. The dark witches over powered the white witches, out numbering them, they thought that they had wiped them out, but some survived. Some remained on earth, and others discovered the time portals, and arrived on other planets.

Alicia and Jessica were astonished, when they saw the town and school buildings.

"What a wonderful sight!" Alicia remarked.

"I suppose its okay," Jessica replied negatively.

"It's our new life Jessie," Alicia said, trying to instil a little positivity into her life.

"You wanted to come here after Elaina said that it was good," Jessica said, complaining.

"You will benefit as well as me," Alicia said.

"We make look alike as sisters, but we don't want the same things," Jessica objected.

"You can perfect your powers, and help others like the time witches do," Alicia explained.

"Sacrifice my life, for the sake of others," Jessica said. "I don't think so."

"Is this Selfish Jessica talking now," Alicia asked her.

"You wouldn't understand," Jessica replied in a manner of fact manner. "It's called self-preservation."

"Oh, my dear Jessica," Alicia said bluntly. "I do understand, it's a case of I am alright to hell with the rest of the universe."

"That's actually quite accurate Alicia," Jessica said sarcastically. "Top marks for that, my clever sister," she said, and noticed that they were at the entrance to their new school.

A new chapter was about to begin in their lives, as another generation of Faber's enter the school of magic, or as Alicia would say, 'Give it a go, mojo.'

Annabella

THE SCHOOL OF WITCHES

The school was no disappointment to either of them, Alicia had a good feeling about the place as soon as she entered the building. Jessica reserved her judgement until she met the school professors, and formed her opinion from seeing them. Alicia has the habit of jumping in feet first, into situations, making her rash and impulsive. Jessica is far more cautious and classed as more sensible, even though Alicia accuses her of self-caring. They had grown up together, with parents Joseph and Marian Faber using their powers for good. Jessica was like her father, very forthright and focused, while Alicia was more like her mother, caring and far too trusting. Their parents prepared them for school, by teaching them what they could about spells, the history of magic, the book of shadows and all aspects of magic, as well as warning them about the dangers of the dark and mystical world. A world corrupted by evil and satanic influence, with dark wizards and witches, doing their best to ruin the universe with their evil ways, led by the devil.

Alicia and Jessica entered their first class as witches, this was relaxation with a difference, using levitation in order to float horizontally to the ceiling. The object was to fully relax lying on a mat on the floor and rising up until they were inches from the ceiling almost touching the ceiling with their nose. Most of the student managed to float half way, others reached the objective, and a few never even left the ground. Alicia and Jessica were used to doing this at home, and so they floated up and stayed up until they were asked to get down. They had successfully passed their first test, by keeping calm and relaxed in the classroom environment, the teacher was clearly pleased.

The next lesson was on magic spells, this required a knowledge of the required spells and using either Scottish Gaelic, Latin or another intergalactic language acceptable by the school of magic. Alicia and Jessica were versed in Gaelic, from their ancestors in Scotland, the cave dwellers who were also the ancestors of Shanice, Crystal, Elaina and Natasha. Luna's family history was a mystery, apart from her parents Oshma and Asha Bassak. Her parents were known as intergalactic nomads, roaming from place to place like new age travellers. Traveling through space from planet to planet, with no aim in life, but to feel totally free from any society or race, but happy doing that.

Alisha and Jessica first encountered the school bullies, when they were upsetting Luna and Maya, they had fixed their lockers so that they sprang open hitting them in the face. Luna was made to slip on the floor by a girl called Lavender, using a spell to make the floor slippery, causing Luna embarrassment. Lavender was a beautiful blonde girl and knew it, she was very vain, everything about her had to be perfect, especially her face, with no spots or blemishes. Her friends Florentine was slightly overweight and Datura was goofy looking with uneven teeth and acne overload, a face full of spots, like an invasion. They made Lavender look good, so she let them tag along like lost pets. Lavender was spiteful and cruel she used other tricks to further their Luna and Maya's humiliation, such as making the bed collapse, and putting frogs in their beds. Lavender was the ring leader with Florentine and Datura, her mean followers who enjoyed seeing others suffer.

Alicia noticed Lavender using her magic, and counteracted her spell, causing her to slip over instead, bumping her head on the wall. She lay on the floor dazed, shouting to her friends who were laughing. "Don't just stand there laughing, pick me up!"

The others helped her up reluctantly, "How rude!" Florentine said.

"Too rude!" Datura commented.

"I am so angry," Lavender said. "Wait until my parents find out how I have been treated?"

Later that evening, Lavender conjured up more frogs for Luna and May. Again, her spell back fired this time thanks to Jessica, and the frogs ended up in Lavender's hair, cold and slimy, making her shudder and shake. She ran screaming down the corridor in her nighty, she was stopped by the teaching staff, but she was unable to explain what had happened, because she was not supposed to abuse her powers. Lavender was given detention with her friends, for unruly behaviour, running and screaming down the corridor at night. The teachers were also not stupid, after all they were once pupils of that school, and recognised the pranks that took place.

The next morning, Lavender had realised that Alisia and Jessica were to blame, Datura had seen them each time a prank was set up, it would not take a genius to work it out.

"Alishia and Jessica will pay for this," she shouted.

"What are you going to do Lavender?" Florentine asked her.

"I don't know yet," she replied. "Watch this space?"

The day seemed to flash by, filled with activities with activities, before they knew it, the evening was upon them. Luna seemed quieter that evening, as if she were troubled by something or someone, but as they persuade her troublesome mind they discovered much more below the surface.

"What's wrong Luna?" Maya asked her.

"The future looks bleak, dark clouds are filling the skies, in the darkness menace exists, and the demons will capture their souls," she explained.

"What is she babbling on about?" Jessica asked.

"She is a moonchild with the power of divination," Maya replied.

"Come share my vision," Luna said.

"She wants us to follow her to a quiet deserted spot," Maya said.

"To do what exactly?" Jessica asked.

"Join her in a séance," Maya replied.

"You mean an actual séance?" Alisia asked excitedly. "Contacting the dead?"

"So, she is a medium too?" Jessica asked. "Cool!"

"You don't have to come," Maya said.
"Are you kidding?" Jessica said. "I wouldn't miss this for the world."

They walked into the dark forest, with their wands raised, shining brightly, lighting up the was all staying close together, all they could here was the sound of night creatures. They had to tread carefully as the ground was uneven, covered in trigs and leaves, with obstacles such as logs and rocks.

"Maya, she's not some witch that strips naked and dances around fires, is she?" Jessica asked.

"No, your quite safe, no stripping," Maya reassured them.

"Hey Jessie, whatever it takes," Alicia replied. "I up for it."

"Alicia, behave," Jessica said, sharply. "Any excuse to take your clothes off, sometimes I wonder if you are really my sister."

"If you have got it why not flaunt it, I say," Alicia said teasing.

"What do you say girls?"

"I like skinny dipping in a lake," Maya admitted. "If the situation calls for it, I suppose I would."

"Jessie walks round the house naked sometimes," Alicia said.

"When our parents are out?"

"That's enough Alicia," Jessica said, angrily. "What I do in my home is my affair?"

"That's true Alisia," Maya said.

"Don't encourage her Maya," Jessica said bluntly.

The girls found an ideal place to hold their séance, a small open area with enough shelter by trees, quiet and secluded, in the open air and not in a stuffy room.

"Okay, take your clothes off," Luna said.

"What?" Jessica said alarmingly. "You are kidding."

"Yes, I am joking," Luna said smiling. "Just my joke," she continued, while giggling.

"Well, I don't find it funny," Jessica objected.

Luna simply ignored her and prepared the ground for the ceremony. She blessed it speaking in Scottish Gaelic, and spreading some kind of herb like substance over the soil, "Beannaich an talamh seo airson an tachartais seo a tha ri thighinn, cùm sinn bho chron mar a tha sinn nar caraidean don ùir agus a tha dèidheil air nàdur." Her words translated referred to the blessing the ground respecting nature and keeping them safe.

Luna produced large candles, enough to make a large circle, the girl all lit candles as instructed, and then they were told not to enter the circle, under any circumstances. She placed a sign of a star in the centre of the circle and asked the girls to spread out around the circle, and wait while she summoned a spirit. The girls didn't know what to expect signs, sounds it was not like a conventional séance, Luna rang a bell twice and then continued speaking in Scottish Gaelic, the tongue of the origin of witches.

"A Spioraid na talmhainn, air a liostadh dhomh, is mise an leanabh gealach a bu mhath leam bruidhinn riut mu chùisean èiginneach. Feuch an toir thu comharra dhomh gu bheil thu an seo ann an dòigh air choireigin." She was asking the spirits to acknowledge her in some way, by sound, vision or another means of communication.

Jessica was sceptical and couldn't understand this strange ceremony that she thought was nothing like a séance, she knew the language as did the others, because it was taught at home with Jessica and Alicia, and at the school of magic.

"This is stupid," Jessica said. "They are right about you Luna; you are a pudding head."

"Jessie, stop, please," Alisia insisted.

At that moment the ground began to shake, they all trembled with fright, except for Luna who was composed.

"Did everybody feel that?" Jessica said.

"Yes, an earthquake," Maya said.

"Sorry Luna you're not a pudding head," Jessica said apologising.

The earth shuck again but with more ferocity, and then a blue smoke appeared in the circle, that increased in size filling the circle.

"I don't like this," Alisia said.

"What have you summoned up Luna?" Jessica asked.

Suddenly the face of a beautiful woman appeared, she was young with dark hair, and hazel eyes, dressed in a seventeenth century outfit.

"Annabella!" Maya shouted.

"Who is she?" Alicia asked.

"She is a witch from the past," Maya explained. "Sort of related."

"Feasgar math nigheanan," Annabella said, meaning good evening girls.

"I am Annabella, you summoned me from my resting place on earth," she explained.

"I summoned you Annabella," Luna said. "I am Luna."

"You know me," Maya said. "This is Alicia and Jessica."

"The future time witches," Annabella said. "The next generation."

"We are?" Maya asked with surprise.

"Sit together on one side of the circle," Annabella said. "Look into your future."

Annabella caused images to occur, of a meeting of two generations of time witches, they were in battle. The new generation came from the future to help the original time witches.

"See how you all have grown, fighting evil with good," Annabella explained.

"I know that this is why you summoned me, you wanted reassurance about your future. Your future is safe and you will be protagonists of your time, travelling in time and space helping others."

"I never wanted that," Jessica said.

"But you saved Luna from being bullied, you are the one who is most favoured for this work, for your mental strength and sustainability."

"In that case, count me in," Jessica said, agreeing. "I am up for a challenge."

"Maya led the way for your friends, please stay safe," Annabella advised. "You must return to school now, before you are missed."

The girls returned to school, the hall was quiet and the corridors were empty, so they crept quietly to their rooms, tip toeing as they went. Maya and Luna said goodnight to Alicia and Jessica, and they parted ways, the sisters shared a room and so did Maya and Luna next door. Fortunately, it wasn't too late, Maya stayed up talking to Luna, wanting to know why Luna was so anxious, and needing help from spirits.

"I kept seeing visions and wondered what they meant, Annabella explain everything that really mattered," Luna said.

"Well, that's okay then," Maya replied. "Did you explain this to the sisters?"

"Yes, on the way back, don't you remember?" Luna asked.

"Not really I was thinking about Annabella," Maya said. "I suppose that distracted me."

Meanwhile next door, Alicia and Jessica were talking quietly.

"Do you like Maya and Luna?" Alicia asked.

"Yes, I do, although Luna is a bit odd," Jessica commented.

"But Maya did explain how the time witches met her, alone at the federation headquarters, acting very strange and Maya was the only one, who could get through to her. She could fully understand what she was saying when nobody else could, Luna trusted her and opened up to her."

"I gathered something was wrong in her past," Alicia replied.

The night became stormy, with thunder and lightning keeping the girls awake, loud claps of thunder and lightning that lit up the room, followed by heavy rain that beat on the windows. Luna usually slept through most things, but her thoughts kept her awake, and when she did sleep, she had nightmares. Maya was tossing and turning unable to get comfortable, Alicia slept close to Jessica because she was shared of the storm, and Jessica was awake thinking about their experience in the woods.

The next morning it was time to learn, an age-old tradition, which was to fly on a broom on a popular circuit, around the campus.

This gave Lavender a chance to attack Luna and Maya, they set traps around the circuit that would immobile both of them. They used hornets and other insects, thin wires and other obstacles, hoping one would work, like making them fall into a muddy mire. They expected Luna and Maya to be novices at flying with a broom, but the time witches had taught them to fly, Shanice also pointed out the things that witches do in races to win. They all had a practice at flying around a field, before venturing out on the circuit, Luna and Maya made deliberate mistakes to look as if they were struggling to fly. Alicia and Jessica flew elegantly in the sky, evidently taught by their parents, Joseph and Marian Faber. Time came to fly in a group, they were reminded that it wasn't a race, just a test of skill, they just needed to complete the course. Mrs Edna Hassle-worth was the instructor, a witch of the finest pure blooded witch family, she was a stout lady, with dark hair and had a haughty laugh, who always seemed to wear long purple dresses. She had a wart on the end of her long nose, which was probably why she was cross eyed, through staring at it. Despite her size she could fly a broom with dignity, and went around the circuit with them, along with teaching assistants. The first trip went well, everybody behaved until the second time, when Lavender set the traps for Luna and Maya. But Luna's clairvoyance saved the day, seeing images of on coming events, using her telepathy she warned Maya, who in turn warned Alicia and Jessica. Mrs Hassle-worth picked up the message and also avoided the traps, unfortunately others didn't receive the message and fell into the traps. Datura landed in the hornet's nest, and got badly stung, her body began to swell up as she was allergic to hornets. Another witch hit a wire and fell into the mud followed by two other unfortunate retches, Florentine got hit by a branch that was rigged up to hit someone, and knock them off their broom. The final trick was fleas in a bag, hanging from a branch that dropped down, landing on an unfortunate victim along with itching powder for good measure. This just missed Maya, who was kicked to one side by Luna, and landed on Lavender's head and body, causing her to stop and scratch like mad. The course ended with Jessica well out in front, but that was thanks to Luna who saved her from so many obstacles, Maya was second to arrive in tact.

Later they were offered a chosen subject to study, it could be separate from their other subjects, outside the school of magic. Maya, Luna, Alicia and Jessica all chose flying a spaceship and gaining a licence, using the space federation academy simulator and then flying a small vessel around space. This gave them the opportunity to do something different, others joined them, making them twenty hopeful pilots. Flying spaceships was a special skill and a good career for some, it was also the way to get about, traveling across the universe.

Since the experience with the broomsticks around the circuit, Lavender and her gang went quiet for a while. Pupils concentrated on their studies, until the holiday time making good grades, Lavender never forgot her experience and swore to pay Maya and Luna back someday. She continued to make the odd comment to them and small tricks in the second year, but it was the third year that Lavender made a big mistake. She was meddling in forbidden magic, the kind that dark witches used, she wanted to humiliate Luna and so she found a spare room one night, and tried to contacts spirits that would harm Maya and Luna. This would put not only Maya and Luna in danger, but the entire school, but Lavender just wanted to attack the two of them, using any means she could.

The girls were in a science class working on chemical reaction, and the association with magical powers, they were informed of the cave dwellers and the meteor storm that brought about their powers. It was passed down through the generations, with the book of shadows as a guide to using such power, and the energy was a mighty force to be reckoned with. It was important for the pupils to know what they had, and to use that power for good, unlike the dark witches, who used it for their own gains. The energy had to be channelled in order to maintain its usefulness, directed by a wand or other instrument as a conductor, in order to be safe. Certain spells were forbidden by the council of witches, spells that do harm to others, change people's shape or form or alter aspects of time.

Lavender was talking through class and upset the teacher professor Godfrey Andrews, who peered over his silver rimmed glasses, scratched his bald head and shouted.

"Silence this is not the playground!" He shouted. "Lavender, see me after."

Lavender and her friends got detention, the professor explained to them, how important the subject was, and that they must concentrate. He warned them about the dangers of not using spells properly, putting others at risk due to bad practice, hoping that they would remember what he said. They were warned about the evils of the dark magic practiced by the dark witches, and about the sorcery of the evil wizards like Merek or Bula Seraph. They were aware of Bula's treachery, they heard many stories of his deeds and of the Lamians, who were serpents from hell, scaly snake like creatures half reptile and half human. But still, Lavender held her séance despite the danger, in order to harm Luna and Maya.

That evening Lavender took her friend to a disused section of the school, and set up the room for her séance, with all the necessary equipment like the table with the Star and letters around it, using a glass placed upside down. She got her friends comfortable and got them to hold the glass with one finger, calling upon the spirits to respond. Speaking in Scottish Gaelic their ancestor's language from Scotland, hoping that their magic was strong enough to contact them.

"Thig spioradan na Samhna oirnn, Cluinn gach Oidhche Shamhna sinn 's freagair Am bheil thu leinn?" Lavender said dramatically.

She was summoning up the god of Samhain, and then she waited.

Shortly after thunder sounded making them all jump with fright; this was followed by flashes of lightning.

"You have the atmosphere," Florentine said. Looking around the room and then outside through a small window.

"Are you sure that you know what you are doing?" Datura asked.

"Of course, I do," Lavender insisted.

At that moment the glass started to move, spelling out words.

"Who are you people?" it says.

"One of you moved that," Datura said "Which one of you?"

"None of us," Lavender said.

It began to move again and spelt out, "I moved it."

"We are witches," Datura said. "Who are you?"

"My name is Nabara," she replied. "Would you like to see me?"

"Yes," Lavender said anxiously. "Please show yourself to us."

"What are you doing Lavender?" Florentine asked.

Suddenly flames came up from the centre of the circle, and a dark witch appeared, a dark-haired woman with a mean expression appeared before them.

"Why have you summoned me?" Nabara asked.

"We need your help?" Lavender said. "Where are you from?"

"I am from the caves of Scotland or Alba near a place called Inverness," she explained.

"We have heard of it," Lavender remarked. "Where the cave dwellers lived and the place where they got their powers."

"How clever of you," Nabara said. "I am one of the eight witches of Teversham, who was killed by, witch hunters, I am a dark witch, one that has been awakened by you."

"We need you to frighten white witches," Lavender explained.

"Just scare them," Datura said.

"Just scare them?" Nabara said. "Not kill them, or frighten them literally to death?"

"No, it is merely a prank," Florentine said.

"I hate white witches," Nabara replied. "I would like to kill them all."

"Just scare them," Lavender said. "That's all."

Lavender explained who they were, Nabara recognised their names, but tried not to look surprised, and then she disappeared, leaving the pupils wondering what she was going to do.

Nabara was one of the worst witches to contact, she was pure evil and cunning, one of the original eight witches of Teversham from the 17th century, who killed men, women and children. Causing havoc in different periods of time, having no mercy or regret, and not to be trusted. Known to the time witches, whenever she appeared to haunt many poor souls, when it came to attempting to kill them. Nabara called on her seven friends to help her, these were the seven other witches of Teversham making them eight. These are Albelenda, Florina, Babeth, Renilda, Rosalinda, Jeliana, Passara and of course Nabara, Albelenda was the leader and Annabella's cruel mother. Annabella escaped from her evil mother and became a white witch, she fell in love with Eric and they had a baby girl called Rosa, Rosa in turn gave birth to Shanice.

The first sign of their presence was a whirlwind that spun around the corridors of the school, knocking girls into lockers and then causing havoc in the library, sending books flying everywhere, injuring children. The professors were outraged, confused by the swirling storm and how it had raged through the school, it was total madness.

But the madness did not end there, much more was to come as Luna could see in her visions, which is why she contacted the spirits and Annabella helped her. Nabara was now in control of their destiny, she and her dark witch friends, ready to ruin lives. The Professors arranged a night in the forest in order to explore the night creatures, led by professor Angus McGuire, with professor Jonathon Lincoln and Lucy Haggle ford taking some of the wizard boys such as Alex Tomlin and Gerry Green. Lavender was excited to see them and made her face up, with make up just to impress, trying to gain their attention. The boys and girls were asked to be quiet, so that they didn't disturb the wildlife. This was asking a lot from such a big crowd, of twenty boys and girls, like asking a dog not to bark, or a cat not to purr.

The night sounds consisted of owl and other creatures from earth, that were brought along all those years ago and bred on the planet, and then they were joined by other creatures on the planet, that seemed a little bit strange. Like visiting Doctor Edward Douglas freak show as Shanice once described it, cross bred creatures of all species. Black bats in their thousands, big moths and alien mammals, fish mixed with birds and frogs with pigs.

But all these creatures couldn't compare to the demonist beast that lurked in the forest with the Lamians, sent by Nabara to attack the children, as she planned to kill all the white witches. The demon beast began to roar, sounding as loud as thunder in the skies, which as the beast approached became louder, almost deafening.

"What on earth was that!" Alicia exclaimed.

"I don't know, but it doesn't sound good," Maya replied.

"Now children stay together," Professor McGuire said.

"Why does he keep referring to us as children?" Jessica said objectionably.

"Perhaps we are to him," Maya said. "After all he is old, maybe forty."

"Listen, it's gone quiet," McGuire said.

"That's not good," Jessica said. "Look all around her."

The next moment a large claw appeared, which grabbed Lucy Haggle field and pulled her into a bush, Jessica ran in after her, followed by Alicia and Maya. They tried to pull the teacher away from the beast, but he was too strong, and then Jessica pulled out her wand. At that moment Maya stretched out her arms and moved her hands about, making sounds and speaking in Scottish Gaelic. At the same time Jessica and Maya shouted. "Obliterate" producing an electrical charge that was seen by everyone, and they destroyed the monster.

The teacher survived with cuts and bruising, she was so grateful to the girls, Jessica and Luna attended to her wounds, While Mr McGuire made sure everyone else was safe.

"This is just the beginning," Luna said.

Lavender was shocked and tried to hide her guilt from the others, but Datura and Florentine knew it was her fault the beast was here, she had unleashed evil into the school with her selfish ways.

"Lavender what have you done?" Datura asked her.

Lavender had regrets about contacting the spirits, she realised that she had gone too far.

But she was unable to stop it, she knew Nabara wouldn't listen to her, so she remained quiet.

They all returned to school unharmed, all but one teacher, who was saved by Jessica and Maya, the girls were ordered to their rooms for their own safety. The next morning, the event was the talk of the school, as the pupil's discussed events over breakfast in the hall.

Information was passed from table to table until it reached Lavender, she listened as the story began to change like Chinese whispers, some things were highly exaggerated and certainly did not match the events, only that Jessica and Maya were very brave, for tackling the beast.

"Lavender, what are we going to do?" Datura asked.

"I don't know," Lavender replied.

"Can't you contact Nabara and ask her to stop?" Florentine asked her.

"What if she doesn't listen?" Lavender asked. "After all she is a dark witch."

"Lavender," Datura said with a shocked look on her face.

"What is it?" Lavender asked. "What's wrong?"

"Your face," Datura said. "Your skin is awful."

"What?" Lavender said with horror and stood up holding her face, she took a breath then screamed as she made her exit out of the hall.

All the pupil in hall, which was most of the school, saw the event and all reacted horrified.

She headed for the bathroom, and looked into the mirror, Datura and Florentine had followed her in, Lavender was outraged and hitting the sink and the soap machine.

"No!" she shouted. "I am so ugly, look at me, spots and lumps."

Her two friends stood by and gasped with shock, they were speechless watching Lavender's drama, suddenly she was different no longer beautiful.

"Don't just stand there," she said. "Help me, I can't walk around like this."

The other pupils left the hall, and walked down the corridors to their classrooms, Luna, Maya, Jessica and Alicia went into the gymnasium for gymnastics. Maya wasn't keen on such events, but she went because of the others, Jessica was the sportiest. After warming up with a few gymnastic moves dressed in black leotards, they were taken on the indoor assault course, they were going to play pirates on the equipment. Their teacher was Professor Delilah Hayes, a tall muscular woman, described as having the face of a horse, with large teeth and a wide nose.

"Right ladies," she began. "Once around the course, starting with horse over to the pole walk along that, keeping your balance. Then the trampoline and off onto the ropes, up them and to the climbing frames, try not to touch the floor, or you will have to go back, and start again. Think of the apparatus as aspects of the ship, the plank, the masts and so on, now off you go."

They all set off around the course, making use of all the equipment, and avoiding the floor, which was supposed to be sharp infested water. Most of them didn't have to go back, but a few did include Maya. She was accused of cheating because she levitated up the frame, and used her magic a few times in order to conquer the course. Jessica completed the course with Alicia, both confidently tackling all the equipment climbing, balancing, jumping and swinging. Lavender was sorry to miss the event, but she was too embarrassed to leave her room, her friends joined in the events and succeeded.

Later as Lavender lingered in her room staring at the mirror, she called out to Nabara to help her, she was so desperate and confused.

"Nabara!" she shouted. "Where are you, have you left me?" Just then, Nabara appeared in a gush of smoke, she was angry about Lavender calling her.

"Why have I been contacted?" she shouted.

"Look at my face," Lavender said. "It is hideous, I am ugly like a dark witch."

"You were hideous before, I improved you," Nabara insisted.

"Well do something about it," she demanded.

"You wanted to be a dark witch," Nabara said coldly. "So, there you have it, warts and all."

Lavender could see that she was getting uglier, with a long nose, a few warts on her face a pointed chin and black teeth. She looked just like a fairy tale witch, the type that most people perceive as a witch, in a stereo typical way.

"Why are you doing this Nabara?" Lavender objected.

"You're a stupid child," she said. "Why do you think, you wanted to be a dark witch and destroy others, so must look evil too."

"I don't want this now," Lavender said, upset. "I just want normality."

"Aww, are you upset now?" Nabara teased her. "Well tough, we are here now to destroy all white witches, with no mercy." She gazed at her with a wicked look on her face.

"And guess who is the first to die," Nabara continued. "A wining girl who is so vein and spoilt."

"You want to kill me?" Lavender said, backing up against the window.

"Well, you are no use to me," Nabara said dismissively.

"You can't, you won't," Lavender said nervously.

But Nabara had already take out her wand, and was pointing it at her. "I hope you can fly," she said. Four floors down to your death, suicide because you couldn't stand turning ugly."

She blasted lightning towards her destroying the window and sending her out of the window with the impact, Lavender began to fall, backwards drifting down. Underneath her was a concrete path, near a grassy area, Lavender was looking up as she went, convinced that she was certainly going to die. Just then, she began to slow down and drift towards the grass, she landed on her bottom, and the rest of her followed gracefully.

"You should really be careful leaning out of the window," came a sweet voice.

Lavender looked up at a blonde-haired girl who she recognised.

"Luna!" she said in surprise.

"Or did you deliberately jump?" Luna asked.

"You saved my life," Lavender said shocked. "Why, after all I have done to you?"

"Because, it's the right thing to do," Luna said sincerely.

After this day Lavender considered Luna a friend, Luna removed the horrid spell that deformed Lavender's face, so she was once again beautiful, but she had learned her lesson about vanity.

Nabara was true to her word, planning the destruction of the school and all its pupils and staff, she consulted Albelenda and the other members of her coven, who were happy to help her with her task, she considered that they were unstoppable.

Lavender confessed to the professors about contacting the spirits and wanting to get rid of Luna and Maya, but she had a change of heart and was sorry about everything, hoping to be able to stay there and not be expelled. Luna and Maya spoke up for her, they were very understanding, but the professors refused to comment at that time. They had the problem of, sorting out the spirits of the dark witches, finding a way to get rid of them. Maya thought of one way of stopping them, by contacting the time witches, they knew these spirits and could help them find a weakness in them. Professor McGuire agreed and allowed Maya to contact them, he had met them many times at the school of magic, he also knew about their fine reputation.

The time witches were at the space federation headquarters, they were talking to commander Shepherd about how Maya and Luna were progressing at the school of magic.

Crystal explained that they would be part, of the new generation of time witches, to replace them in the future.

"I hope they will be as good as you four," he said. "A universe without time witches is unthinkable." This came from the man who rarely complimented anybody.

"I think you will be pleased," Shanice said.

At that moment they received a call from Maya, Crystal spoke to her.

"Okay, Maya we are on the way," she said.

"We have to go, commander, we have trouble at the school," Crystal said.

"Do you need our help?" the commander asked.

"No thank you commander," Crystal said. "Trouble with spirits."

They rushed to the hanger and entered their ship, Crystal instructed Foster to prepare their flight to Palletania, she explained the situation to the others, who were fully aware of the eight witches of Teversham. They discussed strategies, in dealing with them and due to the planet being so close to the federation headquarters, they orbited the planet a few times in order to prepare their plan of action.

At the school, the headmaster Professor Leonard Spencer Jones, called for all the school to attend the main hall, for an emergency assembly. It was in order to discuss the present situation, and try to protect the children from harmful spirits. He organised the older children to watch over the younger ones, and the professors and other staff to oversee them. He indicated how important it was for them to be safe and not stray from the groups that they had been allocated to, and above all to be brave in these hard times. The time witches arrived in time to address the pupils; they spoke of staying close to each other until the problem was over. Classes continued to run, providing the pupils with normality, they would continue with their subjects, as if nothing was happening.

The gymnasium was full of pupils on the apparatus, on the assault course playing pirates.

Others were in the large swimming pool, some learning to swim and others working towards swimming awards, building up confidence, while others remained in various class rooms.

Things seemed peaceful at first, it seemed as if nothing was wrong, but after a while thing began to change. Jeliana and Passara were causing havoc in the gymnasium, the pupils were dancing about in the air, as if they were being juggled, and then tossed on the ground. Elaina was present and saw Jessica thrown about, so she thrust her hands forward, and struck Jeliana with lightning. She hit the ground with a heavy thud, Passara tried to burn the ropes, with some of the girls hanging onto them. Elaina sent water up to put out the flames, and also sent a bolt of lightning towards Passara, knocking her to the ground. She said a few words in Scottish Gaelic, a spell to rid the school of these witches.

"To quote the Beatles," Elaina said. "Till air ais chun an robh thu uaireigin," or get back to where you once belong.

The two witches vanished, and the children cheered and clapped loudly.

Meanwhile, in the swimming pool Renilda and Rosalinda were dragging children underwater. Renilda had Lavender by the legs dragging her under water, trying to drown her. While Rosalinda was doing the same thing to Maya, who was struggling to breath, going further under. Natasha arrived to stop them, using her wand to send the dark witches into the air, and back into the water. Rosalinda conjured up a shark, sending it towards the girls, and Natasha sent that in the air and made it explode. She used the same spell as Elaina used to get rid of the dark witches, and they too disappeared.
The remaining four witches were, somewhere around the school, waiting to pounce on any white witch they could find. No one was safe, and everybody was scared, at the thought that the dark witches were on the loose.

Alicia was going to the toilet with Crystal escorting her, Babeth was watching them, who signalled Florina to follow her. They reached the toilet and Florina managed to divert Crystal, she made animal sounds like a tiger, around the corner. As Crystal followed the sound, Babeth entered the bathroom, Alicia went into a cubicle, while Babeth searched for her. Alicia stayed quiet, listening for any sounds, she was shaking nervously, and she could feel her chest tighten, she felt her heart beating fast. Suddenly she heard a voice, calling her.

"Alicia, it's me Crystal," came the voice.

Alicia opened the door, but instead of Crystal it was Babeth pointing her wand at her.

"Hello my dear," she said. "Oh, you're so sad that it's me and not Crystal, I do incredible voice impersonations, and can even look like her," she said, transforming into Crystal.

"What do you want?" Alicia asked.

"Why to kill you of course," Babeth replied.

"Not today you're not," Crystal shouted and struck her with lightning.

"Where did you go?" Alicia asked.

"To kill a tiger called Florina," Crystal replied. "Florina transformed herself into a tiger, so I got rid of her."

Crystal used the spell to make the two witches vanish, this left Albelenda and Nabara, who could be anywhere. And so, everybody started looking for the dark witches, in every possible hiding place, every building and every room. They had to be somewhere, watching the pupils, ready to pounce, or to fight the white witches, when they are ready to attack, this was very unnerving waiting for that moment.

Some of the girls were playing hockey outside, Shanice watched the match, and noticed the dark clouds coming over them, this was followed by a dark storm. Soon after this, Albelenda appeared, and swooped overhead on her broom. She had created the storm, and began to fire lightning down onto the girls, watching them scatter in all directions. Shanice took out her wand and aimed it at Albelenda, but was knocked to the ground by Nabara, coming in the other direction. Jessica saw Nabara and aim her wand at her and fired her wand at her knocking her off her broom, Nabara steadied herself from the fall, and retaliated. But missed Jessica and hitting Lavender, Maya rushed in to Lavenders defence with Luna also attacking Nabara. This time destroying her and then they turned to Albelenda, who was attacking Alicia, as a united force they destroyed her too.

They all said the magic words, to return them to where they belonged, happy to be victorious over the dark witches.

Later they celebrated their victory, with a fine feast, Lavender was forgiven for her misconduct thanks to Maya, Luna, Alicia and

Jessica, defending her. The time witches could take some credit, as they also spoke up for Lavender. She had learned a valuable lesson in loyalty, and respecting others, she was also lucky to survive from the dark witches. Her friends Florentine and Datura stuck by her, although she had been spiteful to her, it took her a while to adjust to the new Lavender, and recover from her injuries. But whenever she looked in a mirror, it reminded her about what she could have lost. School was changing for all of them, for the remainder of time at the school of magic, graduation was soon upon them, and they needed to pursue their chosen careers.

Luna and Maya got their pilots certificate, and studied meditation and natural medicine, spending time with the guru Bakul Patel and Arlanda from Gudesh. Learning the fine arts of relaxation, meditation, Ergokensis, energetic medicine, Astral projection, pyrokinesis and much more. Alicia and Jessica were already familiar with these things, having grown with parents, who processed great powers, and taught their children well. They concentrated on space flight and understanding science, Physics and astrology.

Maya had been studying earth's history, and had been to various places with the time witches, traveling in time and space. One of her presentations at school was about mother earth and her appreciation for nature, as she pointed out true witches respect the earth.

This went back to the wicca's where the name 'witch' originated, for nature is my religion and the earth is my church, as the wicca's would say adopted by the time witches. Luna gave a talk on clairvoyance and divination, explaining the things that she sees in her mind and dreams. Alicia discussed levitation and telekinesis, and Jessica concentrated on Astral projection, materialization, and bilocation. All together their powers, allowed them to help others, and took them on their journey to being time witches. Maya gained her powers by accident, when she touching a machine containing a meteor with a harmful energy that gave her power but nearly killed her. Her strongest powers are, psychokinesis. (Moving objects with her mind) pyrokinesis (controlling flames, fire or heat) and telepathy (communicating with the mind) she was able to do other things too, like her friends.

The dark witches had their powers too, but miss used theirs, causing harm to others, and dealing with their own selfish needs. They gave a bad name to witches, having the reputation of destroying life, summoning demons and performing black magic. Through the ages people stereotyped witches, as being ugly old hags, who cast evil spells on good people, and flew about on broomsticks.

GENERATIONS OF THE TIME WITCHES

The years went by and the one-time school girls were older and wiser, they experienced a lot from eleven years old, until they were twenty, and completed their education and training. Those years helped them develop into fine ladies, they had developed their powers as witches, as well as their minds, in order to control their emotions and skills. The years moved on, until they reached twenties, and were fully ready to replace the original time witches, they were to become the next generation of time witches. They original team had retired, they all had their own lives to lead, Shanice wanted to do further studies in Manchester, Natasha got married to Doran and started a family, Elaina went to join Angelica at the space federation, and Crystal went home to look after her father Zenith on Aspera. The all kept in contact, and observed the progress of the new time witches, but they had nothing to worry about, the universe was safe with them.

They had experienced the ladies coming from the future to help them. They sensed problems on a big scale from Bula Seraph the evil wizard and the demon creatures known as the Lamians, part reptile part human, like snakes and lizards from hell. Following Bula Seraphs wicked plan to infect planets with his virus, named the Bula virus after the wizard that perfected it in his cauldron, vaccinating himself before visiting the many planets and contaminating them. Thousands died on each planet before the vaccines could reach them from the federation, Bula's army were ready to invade these planets and build a huge empire for himself. And as he was spawned from Merek's spirit, he was doing it for Merek himself, with his own entity, independent to do his own work.

As Merek was agoraphobic and unable to travel, not even Astro travel as Bula could. The time witches only perfected Astro travel after being with the Fostervarian's, they made it look easy and demonstrated how it was done. Of course, Shanice tried it out first, she visited her home, watching her mother using magic for her household chores, the cheat she said amused by her actions. Bula was cunning enough to visit places undetected, he was very discreet, but his ruthlessness found him out and he was usually caught as he was with his deadly virus.

Castariva was his next target another peaceful planet, consisting of several races of people, living together in harmony, until the virus struck them. It manifested itself as a flu like condition which attacked the immune system, but when it reached the brain, it became vicious killing cells and causing the subject to vomit and have aggressive tendencies. This is when they began killing each other, no one could understand it, the death toll began rising, not from the Bula virus but from the murders. Bula was waiting until they wiped themselves out before conquering their planet. The time witches were assisting the space federation in helping the planets, but the virus had even reached them, although they had the antidote required to fight the Bula virus, some still became ill and some died. The time witches travelled to Castariva in the hope to save people on the planet, they had been warned about what was happening there, and to take care. This was a message from commander John Shepherd, who was feeling ill at the time and worried that he may have contracted the Bula virus. But then, with most viruses there was a tendency for paranoia and set off panic amongst people.

The time witches arrived on the planet, it was a hot afternoon in a desert area, with sand stretching for miles, on the horizon was a rocky terrain and what appeared to be buildings at the side of this, according to Foster, the air was breathable and life sustaining. Everywhere seemed quiet and peaceful, with no sign of life, they remained in the spaceship for a while, discussing strategies on how to deal with the aliens and the virus. Although the aliens were expecting them, the witches needed to do quite a lot for them, including invasive procedures which would probably venture into their religious or cultural beliefs. The witches were strangers to them, and could have different beliefs and their own ideas of cultures, although they were a peaceful nation, influenced by other planets around them. Their ideas of ethical or moral correctness may not suit others and could be of a higher standard, depending on individual's views or collective ideas based on religious convictions. After all the basis of earth laws stem from religion, for example the ten commandments, a foundation to be morally good and follow set laws. The body of each religion is to follow a God and worship him, obeying his laws as is written and pleasing him. The same law is enforced by the space federation and applies throughout the universe, so that people keep order throughout space.

They all decided to go along to the city, they thought collectively they could explain their reason for visiting, and they had a favourable reply to their message. Everything seemed good, but Shanice was sceptical, she had seen things before that looked good on the surface, however beneath the shiny surface was rust and obvious decay. Shanice was no pessimist, in fact she was regarded as a blind optimist, falling into situation without considering the danger, but this didn't feel right. The clairvoyant aspect of her powers as a witch may have become a dominant feature, and she was able to see the future close ahead. But she was unable to see images, or hear sounds that would confirm her beliefs, this part of her abilities had not yet manifested itself.

Bula Seraph had mustered his army to attack various planets, he knew that they were weak and unable to defend themselves, and who would dare challenge the evil wizard. The Bula virus was now regarded as a pandemic and strict measures of isolation had been imposed by the space federation, the corona virus of the twenty first century seemed mild in comparison. But that virus only covered the planet earth, affecting the human race, dealt with by various governments around the world, but with a high death toll. Bula's virus was more severe and life threatening, attacking the immune system and brain cells, debilitating mankind. He sent his armies out in great numbers across the universe, their task was to conquer planets without mercy, leaving no one left.

The time witches decided to travel into the city and find the citizens, offering to assist them in any way possible, using their abilities to cure the sick and disabled. But as they got closer to the city, Shanice had a vision of people sick and dying in great numbers. Some were holding their heads and screaming, beating their heads on the wall and kicking out, acting like maniacs as they rolled around in pain. Shanice was naturally disturbed by her vision, she told everybody else what she had seen and they were alarmed.

"This is new for you Shan," Crystal said. "You have developed a new gift."

"Yes, but I don't like it," she replied.

"The Fostervarian's must have helped you develop this," Natasha said.

"Am I going to get this all the time now?" Shanice said concerned.

"Who knows Shan," Crystal replied.

"Premonitions are special," Elaina remarked.

"Not if they are scary," Shanice exclaimed.

Once they reached the city, they started to explore, going in and out of buildings searching for occupants, Shanice managed to locate them eventually seeing similar images in various settings. They seemed to be in a large room, like a big hall, this appeared to be a large building close to them, this could only be one place situated in the centre of the city. They continued walking down the street until they reached the building, and then they entered cautiously, not quite sure what to expect. As it happened, the vision that Shanice saw was correct, there were people lying about on the ground and some were hysterical, beating their heads on the wall and screaming. It was a very disturbing sight, a look at reality as they were living it, in their living hell, unable to function properly, rolling around in pain. Shanice still had the image in her head, like a living nightmare, she felt as if she was one of these hysterical people, that she saw before her.

"Set up the vaccines," Crystal said. "Let's split up into twos and inject them quickly."

They worked fast injecting each person in the arm, and then moving on to the next one, making sure they missed no one. Some fought them others were too weak to fight, Foster and Laptus helped the time witches holding the strong ones down. After a while they were all exhausted treating the patients and had to rest, before continuing and helping more of them. By this time the Lamians had arrived to attack the sick ones, not expecting the time witches to be there, they attacked everyone in sight.

The time witches defended the people from the Lamians, but there were too many to fight, and the time witches were being forced into an almost impossible situation. At this time Bula made an appearance, trying to trick the time witches into surrender.

"Time witches surrender now and you will live," Bula shouted.

"It's never going to happen Bula," Shanice shouted back.

"You have lost the battle, as protagonists," Bula mocked them.

"We would rather be protagonists than antagonists, like you," Natasha said.

The time witches fought on Crystal had administered the last immunisation to a patient before getting hit by Bula's wand, followed by Elaina who slipped off a ledge. Natasha and Shanice were feeling weak and soon collapsed on the ground. Bula was delighted he had overcome the time witches, and sent his Lamians to finish them off. Suddenly as Bula was celebrating his victory holding his arms up and shouting out in excitement, four figures immerged from the carnage. The silhouettes came closer until you could plainly see their green costumes, and the distinctive logos TW (time witches) Bula was shocked by what he saw.

"Surrender now Bula Seraph," one of them said.

At first, they could have been mistaken for the original time witches, but they were a new generation of witches, who had travelled back in time to help the original time witches.

"We are from the future," one said. "I am Luna, this is Maya, Alicia and Jessica."

"Luna and Maya, I know you," he said. "You were children when I kidnapped you on the green planet Grancarna."

"Well, we are older and wiser," Luna said.

"And we are much more powerful," Maya said.

"Is this the great Bula Seraph?" Alicia said.

"Sister, you are so funny," Jessica commented. "The great Bula indeed."

Bula attempted to use his magic powers on them, but they soon counter acted each spell be bestowed upon them, soon he weakened and he was restrained by them using an enchanted rope, which bound his body and sapped his powers. They then attended to the Lamians forcing the remaining army to surrender, as feeble images of themselves crawling around the ground.

"Ultimate girl power," Maya said cheering.

"Let's help the time witches," Luna said taking the lead.

"I will go to help Elaina," Maya said flying down to her.

"Alicia and Jessica help Natasha and Shanice, I will help Crystal," Luna said.

"Tha an àm ri teachd againn sàbhailte" Shanice said recovering.

Meaning, "Our future is safe."

Alicia smiled at Shanice and nodded to her, using her wand to heal her wounds.

"Yes, your future is safe," Alicia said, acknowledging that she understood Gaelic.

"Is sinne an t-àm ri teachd" she added reassuring Shanice that her future was safe."

The future time witches had helped each of the original time witches, Alicia was like Elaina with a bubbly personality, more like an exhibitionist. Her sister Jessica was a little quieter, but reckless like Shanice, professing to believing in self-preservation. Maya was like Natasha and Luna was more like Crystal. All together they were the ultimate girl power or time witches, the protagonist super army of white witches. Luna remembered a lot from her past including being with the time witches, Maya also remembered her experiences especially with Shanice and her family on earth. Maya had formed the new time witches after graduating from the school of magic, she used her acquired skills and powers to help people from the day she got them on Crystals ship called Gena. Both groups of time witches had a long conversation together, and both groups decided to go to the Bermuda triangle together and investigate missing aircrafts and ships. They sent Bula Seraph to face trial at the Space federation headquarters with the Lamians, the bonds remained on Bula until he reached the base.

Both groups of time witches travelled in their own spacecrafts, keeping communication with each other, both looking for potential hazards.

"What is a protagonist?" Shanice asked.

"A leader, hero or heroine helping others," Crystal explained.

"What about an antagonist," Elaina asked.

"Bula," Natasha said. "Our enemy, the worst wizard anywhere, fierce opposition."

"So, good and bad?" Shanice said, trying to figure it out.

"Sort of," Natasha replied.

"It's all about being on the right side and leading the universe into good ways," Crystal explained.

The next generation of the time witches indicated that the original time witches Crystal, Natasha, Shanice and Elaina, would be a hard act to follow. But Luna, Maya, Alicia and Jessica would do their best, and help people around the universe, and in the corridors of time.

Nature is my religion, and the earth is my church.

TIME TRAVEL

It was the summer season on earth, in sunny Manchester where Maya Jay Stokes lived, Shanice was visiting her and Luna who lived with her. Living with her grandfather professor Graham Stokes, her parents May and John Stokes lived around the corner. Shanice was now engaged to George, her parents Rosa and Andrew Finley lived a few miles away, along with many cousins. They had arranged a function for Grahams sixtieth birthday, inviting Natasha, Crystal and Elaina, all were in attendance at a public venue.

It was nice to see everybody together, even Alicia and Jessica attended, as a type of school reunion of the four witches. It was then that Crystal asked them if they wanted to take over their role as the time witches, for the good of the universe. All four excepted the big responsibility, although Jessica was reluctant at first, she felt it was her duty to do something, remembering her oath as a white witch. So, she joined them and later she was glad she did, secretly she did like helping others, but she was not the type to boast about it, just discretely help others, with no fuss.

Professor Stokes stood peering over his glasses, standing at the front of the lecture theatre, looking at the faces of his large audience. Some seemed alert and prepared for his lecture about time, others were bewildered and some came in from the cold ready for a nap. He looked at the bemused faces more than others, the ones who would possibly ask questions afterwards.

"Ladies and gentlemen, I have the pleasure of speaking to you about a subject that affects us all, time. Observe the large clock on the wall to your left, ticking and the second hand going round, observe it for a few moments. I wonder what is going on in your minds at those few moments, why am I here? What else is the professor going to say? And do I really care? Time can be our enemy or our friend, as we race against time for a meeting or a date, you can't be late. Time can be your friend, spending quality time with your family and friends, how many time have you said I wish this time wouldn't end? Doing something you really want to do, and go on doing. How we wish we could turn back the clock to a good time in your life, or visit the past at some point in time, time travel. I can see some of you would like that, spending time in a by gone age, knowing that you would come back here, at this time period."

Professor Stokes had got some attention, as people began to raise their hands, telling him the places they would love to go. Time periods like Victorian England, Roman times and other time periods, some mentioned the sixties and seventies, some even mentioned the future.

"Did you know that it is possible to travel back in time?" the professor asked. "Would this surprise you? Take a plane from Manchester airport to Los Angeles, California, what happens to your watch? It has to be reset for Los Angeles time zone, back in time six hours. Coming home you regain that time, going forward to our time zone or you could go forward again to Australia or Japan. If this is possible who is to say that time travel isn't possible? Is there a way that we might one day stumble on a way to time travel?"

People began to think, working on logic to find the answer, looking at each possibility and reasoning both favourably and otherwise, like searching for the end of the universe, or arguing the existence of God. Professor Stokes presented them with theories, equations, and examples of people who had claimed to have time travelled, such as the time witches.

He left them with that thought, they would decide whether it was feasible or not, there were no concrete facts only theories. The time witches had nothing to prove, they knew the facts, and would be time travelling soon, Crystal and Natasha were sitting in the audience, amused at everybody's reaction, Shanice was sat with the new generation time witches and began giggling, thinking about all the adventures that she had been on. Meeting Blackbeard the pirate, Joan of arc, Cleopatra and so many others, chased by vampires, androids, space pirates, monsters and demons. But no one on earth would believe that, not unless they time travelled or went to space. They were good memories, even though she nearly died a few times, the experience of time travel couldn't be compared to anything.

The professor was answering questions for an hour, and he was surprised to find that no one had fallen asleep, everybody was attentive. The time witches rescued the professor and thanked him for a marvellous lecture, he knew that anytime he asked he could travel with them in time. Elaina joined the others reuniting the original time witches, and joining the next generation, Crystal wanted all of them together to discuss the future. She invited them onto her ship, introducing them to Gena the vessel, giving Alicia and Jessica a grand tour.

"This is my time machine," she said. "My spaceship that has travelled through time and space."

"Brilliant," Alicia said.

"Marvellous," Jessica agreed.

"It's your now," Crystal said.

"Brilliant," Alicia repeated.

"Marvellous," Jessica repeated.

"You two have an incredible vocabulary," Crystal joked. "Of course, I shall formally sign it over to Maya."

"Of course," Alicia agreed. "I can't wait to travel."

"Me too," said Jessica. "Marvellous."

Crystal mentioned it to Maya, who was delighted, and she told Luna. Crystal arranged for Foster to continue on the ship with them and requested that they take Strania and Shimick wherever they wanted to go, either home or with them. They wanted to travel with the new time witches, they knew Maya and Luna, and they would soon get to know Alicia and Jessica. Crystal and Natasha said goodbye to Shanice and Elaina and took the new time witches back to Aspera, on the journey Maya was asked to fly the spaceship. Alicia was navigating, while Jessica acted as co-pilot, Luna was happy to operate the communication apparatus and they changed over a few times. The whole flight went smoothly, everybody took their jobs seriously, and Maya did a good vertical landing on the landing site.

They stayed at Crystals home a few days, in order to find out more about time travel and space journeys, but ultimately it was up to them, to experience it for themselves. It was important to know about the unpredictability of the time portals, and the dangers involved, such as storms, particles of waste, and space junk. Risk to life, such as temporal displacement, atmospheric pressure and other health risks. Bodies that have instantaneously combusted, set on fire or burst due to extreme pressure. These are rare but they do occur, especially when you are not in the ship, drifting down a time portal.

Download and retain, a copy of any time coordinates, for you return trip, so that you don't lose your way, maintain a safe speed and always expect the unexpected. Natasha added that after experiencing surprises, on the way to their destination. Doran arrived to meet Natasha and he told them some of his experiences, he was concerned about the ladies, travelling through time and space. But Maya and her friends were determined to travel in their footsteps, they also saw them travel back in time to help them.

The time witches were ready to go, Maya led the way to the ship, confident that she knew what she was doing. She arranged with Foster to set the course time and destination, Alicia was attentive as co-pilot, in order to learn to do it herself, when the time came. Luna and Jessica also observed, while checking the weather conditions, any obstructions and sudden changes in temperature. Maya did a vertical take-off, followed by taking the ship forward, and heading out of the atmosphere, she steadied the ship in space, and went into hyperspace.

"On course," she said.

"On course," Jessica said.

"On course, Maya," Foster said. "Coordinates set for 1717 AD Caribbean."

"Where?" Jessica asked.

"We are going to the Caribbean to meet Edward Teach, better known as Blackbeard the pirate," Maya explained.

"Isn't he dangerous?" Alicia asked. "Pirates."

"According to Shanice, he was nice to her," Maya said, confidently. "He is tall, broad and a bit scary, but very nice."

"He sounds it," Alicia said concerned.

"Alicia, trust me," Maya insisted. "Well, I need you two to find Amara the Obeah witch outside George Town on saint Vincent Island."

"Is it easy to find?" Jessica asked.

"Yes, I met Amara last time we were here," Maya explained.

"We were discussing the book of shadows and where it had gone."

"Why have we got to see her?" Jessica asked.

"In case she has information regarding Bula Seraph or the book of shadows," Maya responded.

Maya showed them a map with the location of her hut, she described her as a nice African lady, a pleasant witch with a lovely smile.

"She will greet you and feed you, and then if you return to the ship and wait for us, Strania and Shimick will remain in the ship to greet you on your return," she had told them. "Apparently there were missing pages in the book of shadows."

"No problem, Maya," Alicia said.

"No worries," Jessica agreed. "Keep in touch telepathically, okay?"

"I will do that," Luna offered. "It's my specialty."

Maya had landed the ship, in approximately the same place as the last time, when Crystal landed, it was cloaked and therefore hidden from view. Alicia and Jessica had left first for George Town, Maya and Luna left soon afterwards, Alicia contacted Luna telepathically to ensure it would work, as she felt a little insecure. Luna replied straight away in order to reassure her, they had a short conversation, before Maya and Luna headed for the port.

They saw many ships, but one stood out for them was Blackbeard's ship, known as the queen Annes revenge, it was obviously a pirate ship, with the flags that it was flying, skull and cross bones. They were seen looking at the ship, by some of the crew who captured them and took them onboard, and straight to the captain. He was every bit the man Shanice described, a tall, broad bearded man, with a loud deep voice, looking quite menacing, with his pirates' outfit.

"And might these be," he bellowed. "Women on my ship."

"I am Maya and this is Luna," Maya said introducing Luna and herself. "We are time witches."

"Are you now?" he said, looking them up and down. "That has me thinking."

Maya noticed his hair, smoke was coming from under his hat, without a second thought she conjured up water and threw it over him. Luna cringed and looked at his reaction, at first, he just glared at her, and then began to laugh. His crew laughed with him, and he turned to them and shouted.

"It wasn't that funny," he said.

"Your hair was on fire," Maya said. "Didn't you notice?"

"Yes, I did it on purpose to scare people," he replied. "I light it with a match making it smoulder."

"Sorry, Shanice didn't tell me this," Maya said embarrassed.

"You know Shanice?" He asked.

"Yes, she is my cousin," Maya explained.

"Shanice, the time witch," he thought for a moment. "I understand the water now, she did the same, that's why she didn't tell you wench."

"What is wench all about?" Maya asked displeased. "It sounds demeaning."

"You have spirit, definitely like your cousin," he laughed.

"She is mild compared to me," Maya insisted. "I am the tiger."

"Okay, you mangy dogs, get some food and drink for my guests," he ordered his crew.

The ladies sat down beside the captain, and he began telling them about his adventures at sea.

During his conversation, he happened to mention Bula Seraph as a wise wizard, this astounded them, as they knew him as a dark wizard. What was he doing talking to Blackbeard? And why was he claiming to be a wise wizard?

"Do you know who Bula Seraph is?" Luna asked him.

"Oh, she speaks," he said sarcastically. "A powerful wizard who said that he would support our cause, giving us victory over the English and French."

"He is a murderer, evil to the core, serving no one but himself," Luna continued.

"It's true captain," Maya said. "He is not to be trusted."

"Are you sure?" he asked, concerned. "He speaks of me, ruling the seas."

"This is not so captain," Maya said. "He wants all this for himself, to rule the world and then he will destroy you."

Suddenly, a loud knock came at the door, and one of the crew entered.

"A French slave ship has been sighted off shore," he said.

"Let's set sail and get that ship," Blackbeard ordered. "Stay here ladies it won't take long."

Maya and Luna stayed in the cabin, listened to the activity outside, Luna sent a telepathic message to Alicia, explaining everything. The ship sailed across a smooth tide and came face to face with the French ship, cannons roared and there was a lot of shouting. The battle was soon over, the French surrendered, and the slaves were freed from bondage. The ladies were aloud out of the cabin, in order to witness the victory, and see the slaves leaving on the boat to shore. All the pirates were cheering, and celebrating their victory.

But Maya and Luna knew about the history of Blackbeard, and his fate dying at the hands of the English, cut down by them on his ship. Luna had visions of the event, which horrified her, seeing graphic images of the death of Blackbeard. Luna was such a sensitive soul, she cried when she realised, he was going to die, she hated the thought of anybody dying. She felt that Blackbeard, might have been wrongly portrayed in history, books as a fearful pirate, when he wanted to free slaves and hated hypocrisy. Blackbeard revealed what he thought had happened, to some of the pages of the book of shadows. From his perspective, the pages remained on his table when the book went, but the writing was in a foreign language and pictures were of planets and numbers such as eight. He was told by Bula that eight in Japanese represented victory, prosperity and overcoming. He believed that Bula was behind his victories, but Maya and Luna warned him not to trust Bula. They knew it would lead to his death, but Blackbeard never listened until it was too late, when he saw his own fate.

Maya and Luna searched around the desk, but found nothing, fortunately Alicia and Jessica had more luck, when they spoke to Amara, she enlightened them. She used various methods to look into the future, she had seen the pages in her mind's eye, and drew what she saw in remarkable detail. Bula was in possession of the pages and trying to work out the Gaelic words, the images were about souls that had been resurrected. Eight was the victory over death, prosperity was the power, overcoming evil. This was not ammunition for Bula, but a weapon to fight evil, that he was unaware of. Alicia told her the facts on her return from the ship, further more Amara had also seen the death of Blackbeard, but he must have thought that he was invincible or never feared death. Maya was glad that she had met Blackbeard, but sad to leave him, especially knowing about his horrible death. Alicia and Jessica were happy to meet Amara and spend time with an Obeah witch, from Africa now living in the Caribbean islands.

They left earth on their way to another adventure, this time to France 1428 in order to meet Joan of Arc and discuss her visions, she was sixteen at this time.

UNGODLY PEOPLE

It was a sunny summers day in Domremy, which is located in the northeast of France. A young girl was walking in the fields, she had long brown hair, that went just below her neck, a pale complexion, and very slim with green eyes. She was sixteen and her name was in French Jeanne d'Arc or Joan of Arc, her village had been attacked by English soldiers, who raped, pillaged and murdered some of the villagers. Joan had witnessed good Christian people killed, and wanted to seek God for answers to this outrage, she wanted answers to why this had happened. She was in tears until she came across a kind man, who offered to help her, he claimed to be Godly, a catholic priest. So, she told him her tale, he listened intently, and advised her to form an army and fight the English. Me a mere girl, lead an army was her reply, but he said God will be with you. After this she started to dream of angels, visiting her in a bright light surrounded by a choir, speaking of leading the people, fighting the English and defeating them. She saw herself leading the army, onward into battle holding a banner, brandishing a sword, and shouting charge. She had many visions, and dreams that were similar, she was chosen by God to do his will. Her heart and mind told her this, the idea stemmed from this priest, but once it had entered her head, she was convinced that it was real, although today we might say that she was delusional. She could even be suffering from mental illness, hallucinating, maybe schizophrenic or a type of personality disorder, that was triggered by the trauma of past events. As for the priest, he had hypnotised her, being none other than Bula Seraph.

The time witches landed in a field, not far away, Joan was walking to the church, when Luna left the ship and followed her. The ladies thought that she had more of friendly face, and could easily make friends with her, especially on her own. And so, Luna entered the church and walked down the aisle, passing all the pews until she reached Joan. She was praying to God, murmuring words in French, praising the lord for keeping her safe. Luna had her translator in her ear, and Maya communicating telepathically. She waited until Joan had finished praying, before approaching her, she was a little hesitant, thinking of her as this saint that Foster had told her about, saint Joan of Arc she was named years after her death.

"I have come to pray," Luna said, pretending not to know her.

"I am Joan," she said sweetly.

"I am Luna," she replied in French. "Do you live here?"

"Yes, she replied, "Close to here."

"Do you live close by?" she asked inquisitively.

"No, far away from here," Luna said.

"You speak good French," Joan said. "Are you Russian?"

"Yes," Luna said, not wishing to confuse Joan.

"You look like an angel," she said smiling. "Glowing so bright and full of innocents, sent by God with a message for me."

"That is nice that you see me as an angel," Luna said. "But I am a moonchild."

"Is that like an angel?" Joan inquired.

"Kind of an angel I suppose," Luna replied. "I do help people and have unusual abilities."

"Do you have visions like me?" Joan asked. "I see angels and hear voices, messages from God."

Luna thought for a moment, about what she was told about Joan, what the twentieth century historians thought about her, having a mental health condition. Crystal also advised her that people should not feed a delusion, by agreeing with a person who claims to have audible and visual hallucinations. Rather you should bring the person back to reality, by setting them straight, in order to help them through life. But where would that leave those who are witches, with the power to see the future, or have visions things unseen, communicating using telepathy, hearing voices in your head? What is insanity and what is real, define abilities or powers from madness. In Merek's case, he was a dark wizard, an evil man with magic powers, but was he insane or just bad? Bula who was the result of Merek's manifestation, conjured up to do his work, could also be considered mad or bad, but that would depend of interpretation, or opinion.

Luna explained in simple terms to Joan that she did see visions, and she was able to communicate mentally with others. She termed it as a gift possibly from God, in whatever form he may be, making it plain that she believes in a creator of sorts. But told her that nature was her religion and the earth is her church, without going into any detail, concerning God, the bible and other matters pertaining to beliefs. Joan understood, she was fascinated by what Luna was telling her, especially about her origin, from the stars in the heavens, or space. Luna spoke of her friends and how they help people in many ways, Joan felt comfortable and at peace, knowing that she had new friends to talk to, and share her pains and disappointments. She could also discuss how she felt about God, the earth and other matters ponente to her surroundings like nature. Luna needed to return to the other time witches, so she left Joan at the church, and promised to return with her friends, but she was careful not to mention, the fact that they were witches, in case she objected through misunderstanding, the true meaning of witches and differentiating the difference of white and dark witches. Most people of this age saw witches as wicked ugly old ladies, with a familiar like a cat, casting spells on people.

Luna returned to the ship, and explained everything to the others, she liked Joan, but she could understand what the historians were talking about. she was definitely a girl with mental health problems, but so nice and brave, talking about fighting the English invaders, leading the French into battle, guided by God. But one thing disturbed Luna, when Joan spoke about the priest, and how he supported her in becoming a leader, and fighting for freedom and justice. The virgin girl of sixteen, leading an army sent by god to liberate France, she was convinced that she could with Gods help. Who was this priest who condoned her actions, supporting her cause and blessing her sword that she found in a field? It was a mystery to all of them, it was hard to fathom a catholic priest condoning killing. They all slept in the ship that night, knowing how dangerous the area was, especially in the forest, with wild animals about and English soldiers close by. The ships instruments monitored activity outside, and the ship was cloaked, so it could not be seen by the human eye, Foster had shut himself down for a while. Strania and Shimick were fascinated with this time period, suggesting that it was much like their planet, comparing the landscapes. Luna was in bed thinking about Joan, she was concerned about her wanting to fight the English, Joan seemed so vulnerable, a short thin girl and so young. But who was this priest that she spoke about, who had influenced her so much, re-enforcing her delusions about her visions and acting on what God had apparently said or commanded.

The next day, the time witches had breakfast with Strania and Shimick, before leaving the ship to meet Joan, they had conjured up suitable attire for the time period. This was based on accurate information, from the computer, and Foster's memory banks. The time witch outfits would look out of place, and would be open to critics, with too many questions. The ladies travelled through the forest towards the church, looking for Joan, expecting her to make an appearance, but she didn't appear. So Luna looked for her at the church, while the others waited outside, she heard voices coming from a room, at the back of the church. She crept up slowly to listen, the one voice was Joan's while the other sounded like Bula.

"My child you must be courageous," he said. "Fight these demons."

"I will," she replied. "I have the help of angels; they will be with me."

"Angels, do they appear in your dreams?" he asked.

"No, they are real," she replied. "They come to me, and speak of doing good, there are four of them."

"Four, of them," he pondered. "They are witches and ungodly people they will destroy you."

"No, they are angels doing good work," she insisted.

"Where are they now," his voice changed as he became angry. "You must show me these ungodly people."

Luna was about to make her exit, when Bula appeared, she was almost at the door, but before she was able to get there, Bula hit her with a lightning blast from his wand. She was tossed into the air, by the power from his wand, and hit one of the glass stained windows. She remained stuck in the window frame, unable to move, with blood trickling from her head, and arms.

"That's what you do to witches," he laughed. "She is no angel."

The other time witches entered the church, Bula panicked and grabbed Joan by the arms, he held his wand to her neck as they approached.

"Bula, let her go," Maya said, sternly. "You don't need her."

"Stay back time witches, or she dies," he threatened. "And you know I mean it."

He appeared weak as he kept shaking, just as if he was cold, but kept his grip on Joan. Alicia was moving discretely to one side, and Jessica moved in the opposite direction, Bula was trying to focus on Maya, but his eyes were blurry. They signalled Joan to drop onto the floor, while Bula was preoccupied with rubbing his eyes. Joan dropped to the floor as instructed, leaving Bula on his own, at that moment they all fired lightning bolts together, Maya followed by raising him up with Ergokensis, and throwing him right back to the alter. He vanished out of sight, while Jessica levitated and brought Luna from the window, Alicia assisted her in order to prize her off without causing her further damage. There was clearly something wrong with Bula, becoming weak like that, the ladies expected to have an hard fight to free Joan. Joan found her sword, and walked out of the church with the time witches, Joan was upset about the Priest, and so the witches explained that he was an evil dark wizard. Joan invited them to her village, but only Maya was able to go, Alicia and Jessica wanted to take Luna back to the ship, in order to nurse her wounds.

On the way to the village, Maya asked Joan if she could borrow her sword, she held it up and then began to play fight with it.

"Can you use a sword?" Joan asked. "I mean fight with one?"

"Of course," Maya replied. "Fight for what's right, freedom and justice."

"For God and country," Joan said, holding her arm up in the air.

"Can you use a sword, Joan?" Maya asked.

"No, I found this one," Joan replied. "But I would like to, in order to fight the English."

"Why do you hate the English?" Maya asked inquisitively.

"They raped the women of my village, killed the men and robbed us," she replied.

"I can teach you to use a sword, but we don't fight wars," Maya explained.

"You can teach me?" she smiled "That will be wonderful"

"Awesome," Maya replied. "That will be awesome."

"Awesome," Joan repeated.

"Great," Maya said. "That's your new word."

Maya and Joan had some food, and then Maya got two swords, and began showing Joan how to use her sword, Joan soon discovered how to use it. They started to fence until they were tired, Joan found Maya a bed, and before long they were fast asleep. The next morning they were training again, Maya had taught Joan all she knew about combat, and fighting techniques, they spent days doing this. Alicia and Jessica dropped by to see them, they noticed Joan's progress, but advised her to use her skills in order to defend herself.

The time witches were aware that, they couldn't stop forever, but they made the most out of their visit with the remarkable, French girl called Joan of Arc. Just as they did with Blackbeard the pirate, Joan was kind, she was thoughtful although a little strange. They ventured out into the woods, one fine afternoon, Joan knew that they would be leaving in order to help others. That day they made the most of the sunny day, by having a picnic and relaxing by sitting on logs and observing the scenery. Luna who was recovering from her injuries joined them, even Strania and Shimick joined in, although Joan found them strange. Being joined by a couple of green goblins, who were married, appearing as large as life in her local forest.

As it was, Joan was having trouble holding on to reality, the thought of angels, a dark wizard and now green goblins, was a bit much for a mere mortal to grasp. After a few hours of food and merriment, they had decided to walk back to the village. Along the way, they were stopped by English soldiers, who were hostile and started to tease the time witches. They were scruffy men, unshaven and dirty, smelling of body odour, hoping to get pleasure out of the girls, making fun of them.

"Look here," said one of them. "Which one do you fancy?"

"It is difficult to choose," another said.

There were eight men, all as smelly and obnoxious as the other, they got closer to the women, Maya and Joan had swords in their hands.

"They want to fight us men," one said.

"Women fight," one mocked. "Weak and feeble as their men."

They took out their swords and charged at them, Joan and Maya defended themselves, Luna used her Ergokensis powers, to launch one of the men in the air. He hit his head on a branch and landed with a thud, breaking bones as he landed. Jessica did the same with another man. Alicia used her wand to electrify another soldier, sending branches to rain down on others, Maya had fought of one soldier, disarming him and leaving him defenceless. Strania and Shimick used their weapons to fight, bows and arrows, the arrows were strong and sharp enough to penetrate their armour. Jessica and Alicia rose up in the air using their powers of levitation and fire lightning at the soldiers. Everybody fought hard leaving the English helpless, at that moment the French soldiers took over, killing all the soldiers, but one who they allowed to escape, and tell the tale.

The ladies went back to the village, while Strania and Shimick went back to the ship, it was time for the time witches, to carry on to their next adventure. Joan wanted them to stay and watch her battle in Orleans, sharing her victory, but that was not until April 1429 according to earth's history.

"Sorry Joan," Maya said, "But we have to go and save the universe."

"But, how will I possibly win without you?" she asked.

"Joan, you will do this," Jessica said. "God is behind you, and we will know it."

"Awesome," she said, copying Maya and putting up her two thumps in response.

The time witches did the same and all said, "Awesome!"

They said farewell and departed, the time witches were pleased to be part of Joan's history, leaving her to her fate. At seventeen Joan successfully took Orleans with a relief army, and moved on to further victories, until she was captured by the Burgundian army, and handed over to the English. She stood trial, with accusations of heresy, which included blasphemy by wearing men's clothes, acting upon visions that were said to be demonic. She was also accused of refusing to submitting her words and deeds to the judgement of the church. She was found guilty as charged, and on the 30th May 1431, when she was just nineteen burned at the stake. This was an unjust ruling, and in 1456 an inquisitorial court reinvestigated Joan's trial, overturning the verdict, declaring that it was tainted with deceit and procedural errors. Joan was revered as a martyr, and reviewed as an obedient daughter of the Roman Catholic church. She was an early feminist, a symbol of freedom, very courageous as Shanice once said, she was canonized by Pope Benedict XV 16th May 1920 and became saint Joan of Arc. Foster was responsible for tracing her history on the ship's computer files, so that everyone was aware of Joan's history. One of the greatest women in history.

GHOST HUNTING

Throughout history people have been fascinated with the spirit world, searching for answers of the unknown, trying to contact the dead. Ghost hunting, pursuing spirits, sometime to people's demise, wanting to see, hear or find clues pertaining to the spirit world. Some people are said to be more perceptive than others, sensitive ones, children and animals, it is said that you don't seek them, they seek you. Perhaps as some say they haven't crossed over from this world to the next, for some unknown reason they can't cross over and need help. Psychic spirit mediums are said to converse with spirits, with the use of their powers and equipment like the Ouija board. But some warn that this is dangerous, and it should be avoided at all costs, tampering with such things is said to encourage unwanted spirits, even demons.

A university professor called Graham Stokes, related to Maya and Shanice, who was based at Manchester university, was approached by a group of students who were studying psychology and human behaviour. They were looking at the paranormal and human reactions to ghosts, trying to find answers to their beliefs. The professor was keen to help, having experienced this kind of thing himself, with the time witches, and subjected to harm from the dark witches in Inverness, Scotland. He contacted Shanice to join him with his old friend Professor Linus Svensson, who said he would join him, if it didn't involve weird stuff like dark witches, he never got over the cave experience, with the original time witches. His encounter with the spirits of the eight witches of Teversham, certainly unnerved him.

The professor held a meeting with the students, and a few strange people from a local group of ghost hunters, it was considered by the students, that you had to be a little odd to be ghost hunters. These people abused that privilege, Mrs Grace Price was no exception with her staring eyes, her broad face and pale complexion, wearing Edwardian clothes, dark and dusty with black boots. Then there is Henry with his stone wall stare, dark eyes, a yellow tinted skin, he wore a loose jumper and a green corduroy trousers with brown polished shoes. Mable Gladstead wore thick lensed glasses, with her purple dress, intoxicating perfume and dark shoes, with more lines than Clapton junction on her face. Not forgetting her goth niece Abbigail, with her dark lipstick and long black hair, large brown eyes surrounded by heavy eye makeup, she had a long black dress, decorated in lace and wore boots. They made the university students seem normal, even though they were a mixture of fashions from emo to mosh, but it was also how these ghost hunters acted, eccentrics with something to prove.

The meeting commenced with introductions, starting with the students Harry, Daniel, Harriot, Samantha and Hayley, who all seemed quite ordinary, none of them stood out in the crowd. Then the ghost hunters introduced themselves, Mable was the spokesperson, everybody remained silent while she spoke. She had a creepy voice as if she was telling a ghost story, but she was saying how they all met, and a few tales of ghosts. Then there was 'Silly' Sally, so called because she was so giddy, jumping at every sound and claiming it had to be a spirit, which her friends ignored most of the time. Sally had blonde hair in a bob cut, wore a flowered blouse, and short fleecy jacket and jeans.

The professor as chairman had to stop her, in order to make plans to visit haunted places. Such as ruins, manor houses, pubs and asylums, equipment was taken to monitor activity, such as cameras, sound recorders and other useful items.

Shanice was at the meeting, in time to gain the necessary information regarding the ghost hunts, she was eager to meet everybody especially the professor. She was able to catch up with her uncle, sharing their memories together, of their adventures. He also witnessed the resurrection of her mother, from her suspended animation, helping Rosa to readapt into the twenty first century. Rosa fell in love with Shanice's father Andrew, and Rosa gave birth to Shanice. She grew up, not knowing about her mother being a witch, or that she herself possessed such powers. Shanice met Natasha and soon after became a time witch, with Crystal, Natasha and later Elaina, the rest is history or a Legend.

Shanice made her own mind up about the ghost hunters, after all she didn't suffer fools gladly, she had met all sorts of wonderful and weird people. The strangest being Doctor Edward Douglas and his 'freak show' as she called his laboratory, or the strange medium couple who were using the Ouija board to their demise. She was dubious about being with these strange people, but wanted to protect her uncle Graham from harm. So, she decided to put up with the 'weirdo's' and join the adventure, little knowing that the next generation of time witches were on their way. They had planned to see Shanice, in order to ask her about the missing pages, from the book of shadows. Maya wanted to know, in order to find out what was missing and why, she had a feeling that it was significant. Why would those pages be missing, was it something to do with the future?

The ghost hunters set a date, to start their ghost hunting adventure, this coincidently landed on the 31st October 2045, close to the professors eightieth birthday. He had celebrated his birthday on the 22nd, with his family and university lecturers, but missed

Maya not attending. She was his favourite granddaughter, who used to visit him often at home and work. All the students involved prepared for the trip, by packing equipment, note books and clothes, the equipment consisted of:-

EVP recorder

EMF meter

Video camera

Ghost box

360 puck ghost cam

Lights

Lasers

Thermal camera with temperature sensor

Profession equipment operator called Alan Peterson, to ensure everything goes to plan.

The idea is to set up the equipment, have a briefing before proceeding with the ghost hunting, ensuring everybody's safety at all times. Keeping them calm wasn't easy with Silly Sally and her friends, making a fuss, over stretching their imaginations. The plan was to visit a Tudor pub, the first day of the ghost hunting expedition, going down the haunted cellar. They would stop overnight, and move on to a haunted manner for another night. Finally, they would visit an asylum, for the third night, and sleep there on the wards if they dare. It all sounded intriguing, and should I say fun, if that is indeed the right impression for a ghost hunt.

They arrived at the pub, after a short journey, Professor Stokes travelled in his mini bus with his team of students and professionals including Shanice, the ghost squad went in cars, and the time witches arrived, and sent out a telepathic message to Shanice. They arrived soon after, and met everybody in the party of ghost hunters. There were plenty of rooms to stay, in at the King head pub, located in south Manchester. The timber framed building stood out, with the ultra-modern surroundings, like a big black dot on a white board. It had that sensation of enter if you dare, come and scare yourself senseless, the ghost hunters got very excited.

"I can feel things already," said Sally, with her eyes rolling freely around her head.

"I bet," Abbigail replied sarcastically.

"Let's go inside and settled in," Maya said eagerly.

"Give me strength," Jessica remarked. "This is going to be fun, not."

It didn't help that the owner, looked like uncle Seth from the Adams family, sixty-year-old bold man with a fat nose, dark eyes and hunched over, with a creepy voice.

"I swear this is fancy dress," Jessica said known for having no filter over her mouth

"I agree," Shanice said. "Freak show two, as seen in space, with doctor Edward Douglas, and freak show one."

"Come now ladies, we are here to explore the possibility of ghosts," professor Svensson said.

"Quite right," professors Stokes agreed.

The party were just freshening up, as the time struck on a grandfather clock, it was eleven o'clock at night twenty or three hundred hours, time for the haunting. Alan Peterson set up the equipment, in various locations of the pub, with help from the students, who were keen to learn. They concentrated on the cellar, as the main haunted area, as most of the sightings were down there, in that cold and damp area of the pub. Mable would have struggled, to walk down the narrow stone steps, and so she watched that part on a monitor. Henry and Grace joined her in a lounge area, while Abbigail, a Wednesday look alike and Sally went down to the cellar. The students walked about exploring, trying to find clues, all dressed in Halloween costumes. Professor Stokes and Svensson compared notes and the time witches discussed their adventures, with Shanice.

"We met Blackbeard and Joan of Arc," Maya said. "Blackbeard asked about you, Shan."

"I bet he mentioned me throwing water on him," Shanice said. "Because I thought his hair was on fire, but he set light to it on purpose."

"He did because I made the same mistake," Maya admitted. "Someone forgot to mention it, or she neglected to tell me, so as to see if I would do the same thing."

"It was the later," Shanice admitted. "I wanted to see how he would react."

"He laughed and realised that I was related to you," Maya said, laughing. "He was a nice man, but a bit frightening."

"Joan was nice," Luna said. "A very strong-minded lady, very brave."

"Yes, I liked Joan," Shanice agreed. "A special young lady."

"We discovered that there were pages missing, out of the book of shadows," Alicia said.

"Really, I didn't notice," Shanice said. "Was it out of the library?"

"Yes, it was," Alicia replied.

"I think that she is mistaken or confused," Jessica said. "Cosmic dust has got in her head."

"That's no, so is it, Maya?" Alicia protested.

"I don't know," Maya said, not wanting to comment.

"The only way to know, for sure, is to visit the witch who wrote it."

"And, who is that, Shan?" Jessica asked.

"None other than Rodicka Dineham back in the year 1105 AD," Shanice explained. "The book was intact then; I will give you the co-ordinates to travel back in medieval times to meet her. She is a nice lady, a white witch who is very wise." Shanice explained how they met her long ago, and about Bula Seraph abducting her.

The time witches listened intently to the story, and were anxious to meet her in person, after the ghost hunting was over. But for now, they wanted to prove or disprove the existence of spirits, like other strange phenomenon, there had to be a logical answer.

The clock struck twelve o'clock midnight, and the excitement began, Sally was eager to begin, as she went into a dramatic performance as usual. Flapping her arms about, and looking around, she looked as if she was having a seizure.

"Is anybody there?" she asked. "Knock once for yes and twice for no."

Everybody watched her and then looked around, they listened for sounds, but there was nothing. All the instruments indicated, that nothing was there, but Sally insisted that she heard something. The time witches were sceptical, wondering why there was such drama, but the ghost hunters were used to it.

"Who is this drama queen?" Jessica asked.

"Search me," Shanice replied. "Miss annoying perhaps."

They stayed up a few hours, before giving up the ghost as Shanice put it, giving in and going to bed, leaving the ghost hunters to speak to their spirits. The time witches were tired from their traveling, wanting some peace and quiet, in order to rest. The ghost squad ventured on, imagining they could hear things, every creek, every sound was a spirit of some description.

"They are enough to scare away the ghosts," Jessica said. "The crazy lot."

"Jess, don't be horrible," Alicia said. "Let them have their fun."

"Are you falling for their nonsense, Lici?" Jessica mocked.

"No, of course not, how silly," Alicia said. "I know they are crazy, but that's up to them, what they believe."

"Wait until they get a load of us," Shanice said. "Then they will react."

"What are you going to do, Shan?" Alicia asked.

"Nothing," Shanice said innocently.

"Why don't we spook them," Jessica suggested.

"Are you serious?" Alicia said shocked.

"I am joking," Shanice said laughing.

"Well, I am not," Jessica said. "I want to have fun with silly Sally."

"That's tight," Luna objected. "You will give her a heart attack."

"I don't mean a major scare, just a little fun," Jessica said laughing.

"Maybe in the next place," Maya said. "But nothing bad."

Jessica was disappointed, but agreed to wait until they reached the Manor, trying to contain herself until then. They had to be careful, not to reveal their powers, or disclose their identity as time witches, twenty first century earth was still not ready for this. People may watch movies or read comics on action heroes, but they don't expect to see wonder woman or superman performing in front of them. Also, if they were easily shared, they wouldn't visit haunted places, where they are likely to get frightened. Still Maya was concerned about Jessica, and her practical jokes, but Shanice used to be worse and so did Elaina. I wonder how many others would be the same, given the chance and possessing such powers. But it wasn't just silly Sally who was annoying Shanice and Jessica, Henry was equally annoying trying to contact spirits, by holding his fingers on his temples, saying yes and then nodded, telling everyone about, how the spirits had communicated and told him their woeful stories. Although this was a terrific performance, it didn't convince the time witches, as they were unable to detect any spiritual Prescence. The instruments didn't detect anything either, no change in temperature, sounds or anything visual.

When they reached the manor, they all settled in, Alan Peterson the engineer set up the equipment with the students, the ghost squad freshened up before tea. The time witches went straight to their room, also to freshen up with Shanice in toe. While the professors spoke to the owners of the house for more history on the manor. The couple at the manor, Mr and Mrs Seymour had greeted everybody warmly on their arrival, they suggested all having a meal together in their splendid dining room, where they would discuss the ghosts that haunted the manor.

The time witches discussed the oncoming activities, concerning the ghost hunters, professors, students and Andrew the engineer. It was what was considered a predictable outcome, with the entertainment by Sally and Henry mainly, with their Oscar performances. The others knew that they would not be disappointed, finding noises and voices from nowhere, hoping everybody would be convinced by their act.

"So, how long to we endure the ghost squad?" Jessica said.

"Let them have some fun," Maya replied.

"Yes, Jess, they might surprise you," Alicia said.

"We can certainly surprise them," Jessica said laughing.

"Wait for my queue," Maya instructed. "I will send a telepathic signal."

Later in the evening they all met as planned, in the dining room at a long table with Mr Derek Seymour at the head of the table, and Mrs Seymour close to him. Mr Seymour had a mop of short cropped curly hair and wore a monocle over his left eye. He wore a tweed suit and a white shirt with a patterned tie around his neck. Mrs Seymour had rosy cheeks, she wore spectacles and a patterned blue dress, her hair was short and stylish. The ghost hunters reached the dining room first, Sally say next to Mrs Seymour and Henry sat opposite, Grace, Mable and Abbigail sat next to Henry. The students sat near Sally with Andrew, and the time witches sat at the foot of the table. The servants brought the food out, catering for their needs, light refreshments were offered or alcohol, whatever the preference. The service was good, and hospitality second to none, starting with introductions and general conversation. The conversation inevitably led to ghosts, and Mr Seymour began to tell his stories of apparitions, everyone listened to each tale, hanging onto every word that he spoke.

"The earliest sighting," he began speaking a queen's English accent. "Was long ago, round about the eighteenth century, a maid sighted a figure walking down a corridor, and vanishing through a wall. It was a dark figure who has been seen many times mainly in the evening, just wandering the corridors. In the study, people have noticed books flying off the shelf, and papers moving on the table, sometimes other objects have moved. A maid committed suicide by throwing herself down a top flight of stairs, after having an affair with the lord of the manor. She can be heard or seen going down those stairs, moaning and groaning at night."

He continued to speak of many experiences, relevant to the subject of ghosts, and Poniente to the theme of ghost hunting. He evidently enjoyed speaking about this subject, it gave him a thrill, Mrs Seymour merely nodded in agreement, evidently the quieter of the couple. After Mr Seymour had spoken, the ghost hunters began asking questions, you could see that they were eager to find out more, and experience seeing or hearing them for themselves. Especially Sally and Henry, who dominated the conversation, eager to find out more about the apparent ghostly encounters.

The time witches and professors were more sceptical, they had seen and experience strange phenomena, but were aware of people inventing stories, usually for their own reasons or agenda. The last experience with Sally and Henry, warned them to be mindful of fabrication and over dramatizing a given situation.

Later that evening, Andrew was prepared to start turning on his equipment, testing his instruments, hoping to get readings this time. Sally went with Abbigail to the top staircase where the maid fell, While Henry, Grace and Mable went into the study. The professors Stokes and Svensson joined Henry in the study, while the time witches searched the corridor for the dark figure, close to the top stairs. They could hear Sally upstairs, she was talking to the spirits, hoping to get a response.

"Is anybody there," she began. "Copy me if you are there," she whistled and then waited.

"Silly Sally is at it again," Jessica said.

Maya spoke to Jessica telepathically, instructing her to respond to the next sound. Jessica made herself invisible and passed Sally on the stairs, and stood by the door at the top which was once the servants' quarters.

"Knock twice like this," Sally said, demonstrating knocking sounds on the banister.

There was a moments silence, and then a knocking sound like an echo, Sally repeated her knock and once again a knock occurred upstairs.

"Did you hear that?" Sally said, astonished. "That was definitely a knock, in response to my knock."

Jessica transformed herself into a cat, and brushed past Sally's leg on the stairs, Sally screamed as she could not see what was happening.

"Something just brushed past my leg," Sally said. "Was it the maid?"

"No," Alicia shouted. "It was a black cat."

"I heard knocking coming from upstairs," Sally said. "It is worth investigating."

She walked up the stairs, gripping her torch with one hand, and the banister with the other. Everybody who were nearby joined her, watching her enter the room, Abbigail was right behind her, Andrew was present with his camera. As Sally entered the door, she heard a crash and jumped, an ornament had dropped onto the floor. She peered around the room, her eyes examining every inch of it, and then she started speaking again.

"Let me know if you are in here?" Sally said. "Move the curtains, or an ornament, knock or whistle."

To her surprise, an ornament moved across the shelf, from left to right. The curtains started moving flapping about, and she heard more knocking. The cat had returned upstairs, put his back up and started to hiss, looking at the curtains.

"Someone is definitely in here," Sally said. "The curtains moved, that ornament moved, and the cat reacted."

"I am picking up paranormal activity on my instruments," Andrew said. "I also filmed the movements.

At that moment, the door slammed shut, and they heard the sound of somebody falling downstairs and screaming. They all investigated, but no one was there, and then the lights started to flicker, on and off a few times. Sally yelped as something pinched her ear, she held her earlobe and started to moan, this was simulated by someone else moaning.

They all decided to head downstairs, until they caught sight of the dark figure, as it walked down the corridor and vanished through the wall. Andrew was pleased to catch most things on film, and he was eager to edit it later with the students.

Meanwhile, Henry was entertaining others in the study, with his abilities as a medium.

"Right," he said, holding his fingers to his temples, closing his eyes and listening to the spirits. "I am talking to a young lady, who is telling me." He paused. "Yes, I see," he continued. "She appears to be upset, disturbed by the loss of the maid, she said that she was close to her and heard her fall."

Everybody congregated in the study, Jessica and Shanice were invisible, passing books in the air to each other using telekinesis, people were astonished to see objects freely floating around the room. Henry was surprised to see the young lady, dressed in Edwardian clothes sat on a chair, with tears in her eyes. It was as if he had been caught out by his performance, he was as white as the ghost that everybody could see.

"It's a hologram," professor Stokes remarked.

"It certainly appears so," Svensson agreed.

"According to my instruments the area of the room is cold," Andrew explained. "And there are signs of activity over there."

"Is there anything you want to tell us?" Sally asked.

"Yes," said the young lady. "Get out of my house."

"You seem very sad," Sally said. "Can you tell us about it?"

"No," the young lady said sharply. "Just leave me."

"Why won't you let us help you," Henry said.

The young lady stood up, and walked towards Henry and screamed at him, at the same time, Sally felt a something run down her spine, and she also screamed.

The young lady vanished, and a few books fell off the shelves, at the same time as the door slammed shut.

Everybody looked at each other, they were all speechless, all the events took them by surprise, except the time witches, especially Shanice and Jessica the pranksters.

Once everybody had finished ghost hunting, they all had supper and retired to bed. But activities didn't finish there, the time witches wanted to make certain, that there was nothing harmful at the manor. Shanice and Jessica were the main instigators, of the pranks played on the ghost hunters. But some of it was also due to Alicia, and Maya, in order to add credibility to the ghost hunting, such as the young lady, thanks to Alicia. Jessica decided to call on Sally, by knocking on the door twice, and waiting for her to look down the corridor before entering, she was invisible and once inside, she could wait until Sally was in bed and play her up. This worked well, she blew in her face, whispered in her ear and stroked her arm, before quietly leaving the room, after she had fallen asleep.

Sally spoke about it at breakfast, she was keen to share her experience, and she had gained a captive audience. Henry was competing, not to be out done by Sally, he spoke about activities with ghosts. The pair of them were busy, trying to express their thoughts, and feelings, oblivious to the rest of the ghost hunters. So, everyone else either listened or spoke about something else to each other, Shanice and Jessica were laughing about the pranks. Henry did say, it was once of the most amazing experiences, he had ever had. As for Alicia, she enjoyed playing the part of the young lady and whispering in his ear.

They left the manor after breakfast, thanking the Seymour's for their hospitality, and kindness during their stay. They now had to take a journey further north to a remote area outside greater Manchester, this time they were going to view an asylum. This mental institution was used from as early as the nineteenth century, to house mental health patients. There is word of it being, haunted by some of the patients, restless and lost souls. Those that could be said to have broken wings and lost souls, those who are difficult to help, due to their mental conditions. It's said that you can hear them, groining and screaming all through the night. Before medication was manufactured, they had to use alternate methods of keeping patients under controlled, today such methods would be considered cruel and barbaric. Straitjackets were used and padded cells, ice cold baths and twisting wet towels around the patient's neck as a form of restraint. Later in the twentieth century they included electric shock therapy, forced drugging and even lobotomies, these were all legitimate in Lunatic asylums, as they called them. As for accommodation they were overcrowded, and short of beds, accommodating over two thousand patients. Mental illness was regarded as a stigma, people shyer away from such patients due to a lack of understanding, even today people fail to understand mental illness. Expressions like send them in the Lunny bin are heard, Luna means moon it is said that the full moon makes them worse. On this particular night it just happened to be a full moon, ideal for ghost hunting, and this Lunatic asylum was popular for ghost hunting.

They arrived after having a meal at a local café, some of the party brought snack and drinks with them to the asylum. They entered the building nervously, having studied it dark and cruel history, the walls and floors that patients had crashed upon, each area told a story of terror, you could almost see staff dressed in white uniforms. Some of the so-called unruly patients in cages, others with cuts and bruises, scars from bloodletting.

Shanice was already feeling nauseas, her mind drifted back to doctor Douglas freak show. Although the building was different, she couldn't help thinking of his cruel experiments and maimed creatures, in glass cabinets and cages. The time witches all felt for the patients, and the inhumane condition that they lived in. They had been brought up to respect life, and during their schooling, they were told to protect the weak and those less fortunate than themselves, so this came as a shock to them. They had all brought sleeping bags with them, in order to rest there, but the place was cold and damp, certainly not a place to stay for any length of time. It seemed everywhere they looked they could see white tiles on the walls, and some of the bedframes remained, it was if the patients never left.

The group stayed together throughout the tour, until nightfall, there was an electric storm where the lightning lit up some of the rooms. Each clap of thunder made some of them jump, especially Sally as she continually said. "What was that?"

But it wasn't until the end of the tour that things began to happen, by this time the time witches were fed up with Silly

Sally saying. "What was that, did you here that?" and "Something touched me."

Henry was in his own world he had gone almost catatonic.

"Yes," he said to himself or some spirit. "I know," his eyes were staring and then he spoke to the party.

"He wants you to know, he has been treated badly," he said. "He is not happy."

"There are other voices of protest, complaining about their activity, desperately crying for help", Henry said, concerned.

"Stop," shouted Jessica. "Just shut up."

Henry looked shocked at her response, while everyone else just looked at Jessica with disbelief, Henry had his mouth open and was clearly mouth breathing.

"I have had enough of your stupid performance," Jessica commented.

"Jess, really," Alicia said.

"She is right," Shanice agreed. "You and Sally are acting so dramatically."

"That was very subtle," Mable said. "You hold anything back do you child."

"I am not a child," Jessica insisted.

"You are a sceptic," Sally remarked.

"I am a realist," Jessica said. "I am scientific and more interested in fact than fiction."

"Jess, we don't want to upset the group," Maya said. "We each have our own beliefs, respect others." Maya was trying to calm the situation down.

"She is only saying, what we all are thinking deep down," Samantha said.

"And what is that?" Henry asked.

"That you lot are frauds," Hayley said boldly.

"So, what are you doing here?" Abbigail asked, "If you don't believe."

"For our studies," Samantha said. "Your reactions appear to be staged."

"What about the manor, all them floating books and the young lady?" Grace asked.

"Yes, we all witnessed that," Sally commented.

"Yes, but was that staged?" Jessica asked. "How much actually happened?" she asked knowing most of it was the time witches' pranks.

"Jess, no one can answer that one," Alicia said, knowing that if they admit it was a series of pranks, they would have to reveal who they were. So, she sent a telepathic message to Jessica.

"Okay, I admit you are right about that Grace," Jessica said, taking humble pie.

"Let's just put this behind us," Sally said. "And do what we come here for."

At that moment something pulled at Sally's jumper, and forced her to the ground.

"What was that?" Sally said, struggling to her feet.

"Stop it," Maya said to Jessica.

"It wasn't me," Jessica insisted. "I am nowhere near her."
"Is it you, Shanice?" Alicia asked.

"No way," she forced herself down.

As Alicia spoke, she was pulled down, this time they all heard screaming coming from one of the wards, Alicia had banged her head on the concrete floor, blood was trickling from her forehead.

"Put the glasses on Shan," Maya said, meaning glasses that could see invisible objects.

"What are those?" Henry asked.

"Special spectacles," Shanice replied, seeing a woman on the floor.

The lady was a patient trying to get up, by pulling at each of the party in turn, she had been crawling on the floor, around their feet. Shanice bent down to talk to her, but the lady was confused, and just babbled incoherent words. Suddenly, two of the students, Harry and Daniel, started running down the corridor, they claimed to have seen a figure in the distance, not far behind was Harriot, Samantha and Hayley. They followed the corridor until they came to a padded cell, they entered the room and the door shut behind them. When Hayley tried the door, it was jammed shut, and they were trapped. The sound of moaning was heard by all of them, and the light started flickering, one area of the room went cold, the students felt uneasy and all experienced goose bumps.

"What's that noise?" Samantha said, with a quivering voice.

"It sounds like moaning," Hayley replied.

"I don't like this," Harriot said nervously.

"Something is pushing me," Harry said.

"Are we really stuck?" Daniel asked.

"Yes, it's locked," Harry replied, pushing and pulling the door.

"What do we do now? Samantha asked her friends. "How do we get out?"

"I hope the light doesn't go out," Harriot said watching it flicker again.

"Someone will rescue us," Daniel said, confidently.

"You think?" Harriot remarked, "I hate the dark."

"Let's huddle together," Hayley suggested.

"Good idea," Samantha replied and closed in on the group. Suddenly the moaning seemed to become louder, and the room was colder, they could feel a cold breeze around them, like somebody breathing close by.

"Who is breathing on me?" Harriot asked nervously.

"Not me," Harry said, which was echoed by each of them. The moaning stopped and was replaced by screaming, it sounded like a woman, Harriot screamed in reaction of the scream. The light went out and then on again a few seconds later, this time the woman appeared in a straitjacket with piercing eyes and long scraggly hair. She was right next to them, her face was close to Harriot, and she was breathing down her left ear.

"Oh my god," she shouted going into hysterics, "Ew gross."

"Is she a ghost?" Daniel asked.

"She looks so real," Samantha said.

"Andrew need to see this," Harry commented. "A real apparition."

Hayley was comforting Harriot, and at the same time staring at the ghost in disbelief, her mind was trying to rationalise the situation. None of them could quite believe what they saw, it was no trick, no hologram, a true vision. They could all see it, screaming at them and trying to break loose out of the straitjacket. They were even concerned that she might do too, she seemed so strong trying to break free.

They continued to watch her struggling, and then heard a ripping sound, it sounded loud, the students looked at each other. At that moment the door opened, and Maya was at the door, she had seen them enter the room.

"Having trouble?" she asked. "Is that a ghost?"

"Yes," Harry replied. "Where is Andrew, he needs to see this?"

"I am here," Andrew said clasping his camera.

They all left the room and Andrew began filming, hoping to capture the ghost on video. Eventually she vanished leaving them all bewildered, but the moaning and other sounds continued, in all directions. Sally was excited by it all and Henry was conversing with all kinds of ghosts, in fact the whole atmosphere was amazing, at the same time tragic. It was tragic, because of the things that were happening to the poor patients, in torment. How strange the party must have looked, to the patients, dressed in Halloween costumes. Dressed as zombies, witches, vampires, beetle juice and the Adams family. Abbigail was Wednesday from the Adams family, professor Svensson was Fester, Mable was Morticia and Gladys was herself. The students were mainly zombies, time witches were witches of course, and professor Stokes was a wizard. Harry was Beetle juice, wearing a black and white striped outfit, with a creepy face and wild hair style. It was nice to see them dressed up and making an effort to get along, but probably not appropriate for the asylum. It begs the question, who are the mad ones, the patients or the visitors?

This day, which was coming to an end, was the most successful for ghost hunting, although the time witches enjoyed, the manor and their pranks.

Shanice supplied a few of the time witches with her special glasses, in order to avoid patients from crashing into them, when they were running at them. It would have been pointless sharing the glasses with non-witches, as they would not be able to see through them without special powers. So, the time witches looked out for them, making sure that they were safe. Henry tried looking through them, and so did Sally, but all they could see was blurred images, and nothing unusual. A male orderly was seen dragging a woman by her hair, who was stopped by Alicia hitting him with a lightning bolt. Most of the patients had shaved heads and loose clothing, tops and trousers of some kind. Unfortunately, Alicia had exposed herself as a time witch, and so each of them had to admit they had abilities or powers as true witches.

"I thought witches were ugly," Hayley commented.

"As you see, we are not," Jessica said. "White witches are good looking, friendly and kind."

"It would seem so," Harriot said, standing beside Hayley.

"You have magic powers?" Sally said. "What can you do?"

"I can make things appear; I can make objects move across a room," Jessica said.

"Like books in a library?" Sally said, "Or pose as ladies as ghosts?"

"That was me as the lady," Alicia admitted. "I played that prank."

"They were playing you up, Sally" Maya said. "We all have similar powers, but usually use them for good."

"Well, you certainly fooled us," Henry admitted. "Very convincing."

"You ought to work with us," Sally said. "Imagine our powers combined."

"We would, but we have to save the universe," Alicia said.

"Now, where have I heard that before," Shanice said. "I know, I used to say it."

They all left the asylum, and passed the grave yard, they could still hear the sounds of moaning, screaming and shouting, as if they were still on the wards. They travelled from the asylum an hotel close by, hoping for a good night's sleep, without seeing ghosts.

Shanice was talking to the time witches about Rodicka Dineham, advising them to visit her timeline around 1105 AD, in order to find the missing pages in her book of shadows. When the book would have been intact, and find out its secrets, and ask Rodicka if she remembers anything about what she had written. The next morning, they had breakfast and said goodbye to the ghost hunters, Sally had mentioned again about working with the time witches. Jessica didn't respond neither did Shanice, once was enough with silly Sally and Henry, Alicia smiled Maya nodded and

Luna was off with the fairies as usual. After the ghost hunters had left, professor Stoke took the everybody home. The time witches left Shanice's home the next day, and returned to the spaceship. Maya keyed in the coordinates for their journey back in time, 1105 AD to see Rodicka Dineham.

INHERITANCE

It was a fine day in the north of England, during the reign of Henry 1 a Norman king who ruled England. Edgar ruled Scotland during this period, Rodicka Dineham lived on the border of Scotland and England which was divided by Hadrian's wall. Rodicka lived in a cottage near woodlands, a few miles from the hills of Scotland, far from the Normans reach. She spoke mainly Scottish Gaelic, and also wrote in the language, in her book of shadows. The book was always beside her on a table in the lounge, she was visited by the original time witches in the summer of 1105 AD, and showed them her book. Rodicka was a direct descendent of the white witches of Inverness, the cave dwellers, some of the information was passed down from them. She had placed a spell on the book, in order to protect its content from getting into the wrong hands, such as the dark wizards and witches.

Rodicka was said to be very wise and a clever witch, although she looked quite plain, she had kind blue eyes and red cheeks, she was approximately forty years old. She was slim and healthy, and lived alone although she had a cat called Rubin. Her cottage was full of hand carved wooden furniture, and hand embroidered cushions. The kitchen was a typical, country style with plenty of pots and pans, and always a pie in the oven or other products that she baked.

She was carrying her basket, and walking into the forest when she heard a strange noise coming from near the cottage. She had heard it before, but couldn't recollect where from, So, she headed back across the narrow pathway.

As she got nearer to the cottage, she looked around for signs of life, she felt eyes on her. Her instinct was to run inside the cottage, her cat Rubin followed her in, and Rodicka bolted the door. She sensed the presence of people, and pulled out her wand, and stood hiding behind the door. After a few minutes there was a knock at the door, Rodicka hesitated she could feel her heart beating fast. She had been abducted recently, by the dark Bula Seraph, and his demons, was he back again she wondered. She clutched hold of her wand, and began sweating, her whole body was quivering, perhaps he would kill her this time for the book. Somebody knocked again, and tried the door, she wondered what to do, all kinds of spells come to mind. And then she came up with an idea, transformation, turning the subject into an animal like a rabbit or toad. It could work, it was possible, and it wouldn't harm the person. She didn't want to hurt them just take away their means of attack, in order to defend herself. But then she heard a young women's voice, speaking to her on the other side of the door.

"Rodicka, are you there?" she asked.

But Rodicka thought it might still be, the wizard transformed as a woman, and ignored the voice.

"Rodicka, we are time witches." The voice said. "Please open the door."

Rodika's mind was racing, she could hardly think straight, too many thoughts had flooded her head at once.

"Rodicka, I am Maya cousin of Shanice who you met recently." Maya said.

"And I am Jessica Elaina's cousin," Jessica said.

"I am Alicia, Jessica's sister and Elaina's cousin," Alicia said.

"I am Luna, the moonchild and part of the new generation, of time witches," Luna explained.

Rodicka pulled the lock and opened the door slowly, she looked at their logos on their costumes and smiled, with an expression of relief on her face.

"Time witches who were here last year, those who rescued me," she commented.

"We realised that Shanice chose 1106 AD to arrive here after they had been," Maya said.

"Come in ladies," she said, kindly. "Sorry about my behaviour, but I thought you might be the evil wizard, Bula."

"We heard about your abduction, and how our relatives rescued you," Maya said.

"Yes, it was quite an ordeal," Rodicka admitted.

"We understand that you are related to the cave dwellers of Inverness?" Maya asked.

"Yes, Alana is my ancestor," Rodicka explained and told the story of the cave dwellers.

The time witches listened intently as she told the tale of Samhain, the human sacrifice and the battle of the witches. She explained that the white witches were nearly extinct, and only survived by going into hiding, some completely disappeared. The time witches explained that the missing witches, went to another planet and multiplied. Like Aspera where Crystal lives, or were the school of magic is today on Palletania, some exist on Rahattelon. Rodicka was fascinated knowing about the future, and of the white witches surviving, the tragedy of the witch wars long ago. Perhaps Alana was one of them, it would be interesting to know, perhaps the time witches could find out.

Rodicka provided her guests with food and drink, while they continued to discuss their history, Maya explained that Shanice's grandmother was brought up by dark witches. But Annabella hated them and their cruelty, they were the witches of Teversham. Annabella married Eric and had a daughter called Rosa, she survived the seventeenth century, preserved in some kind of jell, and was revived or resurrected in the twenty first century. She then gave birth to Shanice, who became a time witch. Rodicka spoke about the pictures on the cave walls of aliens, the pictures of the witch's power as demonstrated by them. Which included levitation, Ergokensis, telekinesis, and much more, all copied into the book of shadows, or were they, these were some of the missing pages. Maybe there was more answers to the origin of the witches' powers, right there on the cave walls.

It took days to go through the book looking for clues, Alicia and Jessica went on walks to the woods and as far as the Scottish hills, while Luna and Maya scanned through each page of the book methodically. They slept in the ship close by, using the computer to fill any gaps in history, and keeping Strania and Shimick informed, eventually Rodicka did enter the ship and met the goblins. Even though she had experienced a lot of magical things, nothing was more surprising than them. And so, Strania and Shimick told her the tale of the green planet of Grancarna, and their adventures there. It was clear that they would need to visit the caves in Scotland, in order to find and examine the pictures. So that, they could discover their inheritance from their ancestors, and fill in the missing links. The time witches said goodbye to Rodicka, hoping to meet her again at some point, providing her with the relevant information. She had got close to everyone, and wanted them to stop longer, but Maya spoke the words of Shanice.

"We have to go; we have to save the universe," Maya announced.

"Awesome," Alicia remarked.

It was a hard decision, regarding when to go to the caves, which time in history was best to view the cave art. It was considered that, going soon after the images were drawn on the wall, fresh and clean. This would have been, soon after the celebration of Samhain, and before the battle of the witches. But this was a dangerous time, for the white witches who were outnumbered, by the dark witches. The date had to be chosen carefully, Samhain was 31st of October now, known as Halloween, the time witches surmised 5th November 52 BC or close to that date, as the battle of the witches would have taken place, shortly after they gained their powers, during the time of the meteor storm. Apparently, the affects were quite severe, and all the survivors of the storm, were rendered unconscious. A release of gas had knocked them out, followed by a type of gamma ray that provided them, with a type of super power. This was the introduction of magic/Magick, that the witches possessed, from there, they developed their skills until they were masters of their art. But unfortunately, the cave dwellers divided, one group became white witches, much like druids. and the dark witches became evil and selfish.

Murdina the leader of the dark witches, waged war upon the white witch leader Gabbran, and the battle began for supremacy.

But as the dark witches headed for victory, Murdina insisted on executing all the white witches, hunting them down and killing them. She thought that she had killed them all, but a small group escaped, and somehow found themselves on a new world in the galaxy.

Apparently, this remains a mystery, as did the origin of the planets, that collided to cause the meteor storm. According to the druids it was the gods, who were angry about a human sacrifice, her death should never have happened, when she fell over the cliff. Murdina had got her by the hand, leading her to the alter, when the girl fought her and fell backwards over the cliff, and to her death, crashing down onto the rocks.

The time witches landed at the foot of the cliffs, close to where Crystal had landed the week before. Maya asked Strania and Shimick to stay out of sight, in case they frightened the tribes of cave dwellers, or accidently expose them as white witches. The time witches left the ship with the appropriate attire, suitable for the period, and according to historical records, provided by Foster and the computer's memory banks.

"I have a few photographs of the other time witches, dressed in similar clothes," Foster said.

"That would be useful," Maya said gratefully.

"Be careful," Strania said concerned.

"There, there," Foster commented as he did in any crises, known as pre-set statements of emotion.

"Thanks Foster," Alicia said.

Shimick had tears in his eyes, and he was comforted by Strania his wife, as they waved goodbye to the time witches.

They could feel the see breeze, sweeping across the beach, and blowing their long dresses. They pulled up their hoods, in order to cover their faces from the drifting sand, shielding their eyes from the sun. They followed a dirt pathway to the caves, following a map that Crystal drew when she was there, she had marked the cave where the white witches lived. They entered the cave, acting as if they were part of the family, speaking in Gaelic, people offered them food. Most of the cave dwellers were friendly, letting them wander around the cave. It took a while before they met one of the artists, drawing on a wall, he did strange shapes and symbols, which oddly enough had the crossed eights on it.

"Dè a tha sin?" (What is that?), Alicia asked.

"Chan eil fios agam," (I don't know) the young man replied.

"Càite am faca tu e roimhe?" (Where have you seen it before?), Alicia asked him.

"Ann mo cheann" (In my head) he said pointing to his head. "An do rinn thu tuilleadh dhealbhan?" (Have you done any more pictures) Jessica asked.

"Tha, thall an sin leis an fheadhainn eile," (Yes, over there by the others), he replied.

The time witches wasted no time, they immediately followed where he had pointed further back in the cave, hoping to find what they wanted.

After looking at all the drawings, they began to think that the other artwork was in the other caves, where the original time witches hadn't looked. But it was risky and they were worried they might be exposed, it meant being so careful and not standing out. But having said that, they could listen in on conversations, and find out about prebattle talks. It was all about strategy, careful planning and playing a game of chess, thinking moves ahead, in order to succeed. They entered the other caves Maya went with Luna, in one cave, Alicia and Jessica in the other cave. Murdina was in the first cave discussing the battle, getting very loud and excited, her long scraggy hair was waving about. Her friend Fenella was trying to calm her down, but she only made her worse.

"Fenella, listen to me," Murdina shouted. "We will defeat the white witches and then I will destroy them and their children, the white witches will be no more."

"What kill them?" Fenella questioned her.

"Yes, every last one with our new powers," Murdina said.

She received a great cheer from the dark witches, who encouraged her to say more.

"The white witches are our enemy, they have no right to be here, they are useless cowards," she shouted. "Death to them all." During their time in the caves, they felt very uncomfortable, Maya and Luna who were close to Murdina, listening to her awful cackle. Constantly playing with a lump on her log bent nose, or brushing her hair back, and spitting on a wooden doll. She picked up a stick, and pointed it in the direction of a large lady, bending over and, shot lightning out of it.

"Do you like my wand?" she said cackling again.

The time witches explored the caves, Maya and Luna found a few things, that showed that some had clairvoyant powers, drawing picture on the walls about the future. Like the young man in the last cave, but the best find was discovered in the last cave, that Alicia and Jessica were at. Someone had drawn an alien, and a spaceship like the time witches craft, it was uncanny and so detailed. They made discrete enquiries, only to find that it was, the same artist who drew the pictures in the other caves. He was the clairvoyant who could see into the future, he was a prophet with the ability of divination. He even drew the time witch logo, saying that these were prophets and savours from another world.

The time witches sensed hostility, they knew that things were getting worse in the caves, Murdina had proven this with her spiteful tongue. Alina had been in the cave, and heard her talking, she ran back to Gabbran and reported back to him.

"Gabbran, the dark witches are about to make was on us," she said anxiously.

"Let them come," he said calmly. "We will be ready."

Alina's husband Barra stepped forward, he was also concerned about the dark witches and their threat of war. He knew of them dabbling with the occult, demonist practices that was against their druid beliefs.

"Gabbran, they are dangerous and could easily destroy us," he said desperately.

"Barra, we are ready for them, Samhain will be with us," Gabbran said.

Samhain was the God that they followed, little knowing that Samhain had become part of the darkness, and led Murdina to his evil ways, Samhain became the lord of darkness.

Dagda was the more favoured god, he was considered fair and genuine, which was revealed later. He took care of his people, and gave the artist cave dweller his visions.

Tabbron, was the youth in question, Dagda came to him in a dream, he informed the youth about Samhain and the dark world, which he drew on the cave walls. He portrayed Samhain in a fire, a light in the darkness, with monsters all around him. This was quite disturbing as the druids had looked up to Samhain, prior to the meteor storm and considered that was due to Samhain's anger. This was the turning point of the druid faith, and the corruption of their god, resulting in the segregation of the cave dwellers. The power of the witches was the final result of Samhain's corruption, in causing darkness against light, dark witches against the white witches. It wasn't long before the war broke out, the dark witches became hostile, and attacked the white witches using their powers. They were strong and fierce, having no mercy, they used every kind of power they had, to destroy the white witches. It became dark times for the innocent white witches, many lives were lost, men, women, and children were slaughtered. They also destroyed the art work, removing all evidence of their deed's and of prophecies. Nothing was to remain, no evidence that the white witches existed, even Gabbran was killed by Murdina, as a demonstration of her strength.

The time witches tried not to get involved, but they couldn't help defending the white witches, so they began fighting. Maya was confused about Tabbron's prophecy, who exactly rescued the white witches, and took them to other planets like Palletania or Rahattelon? She discussed it with the other time witches telepathically, speaking in English, hoping that nobody was telepathic.

"What does this all mean?" she asked. "White witches rescued by who?"

"My god, Maya," Alicia replied. "We are the rescuers, it's obvious, our ship and we are here."

"That's why the paintings were destroyed," Jessica said.

"That's what I have been sensing all along," Luna explained.

"I saw this image time and time again, the white witches vanishing, and appearing elsewhere on a different world."

"They escaped on our ship," Maya said. "Quick, no time to lose, lets rescue them."

Alicia and Jessica formed a diversion, by creating a large colourful bubble in the air, the dark witches were distracted and the time witches took the white witches back to their ship. Murdina managed to pop the bubble, and then noticed the escapees, she tried to chase them, but she was stopped by a flock of seagulls, desperately she tried to fight her way through them, but she was too late. The ship had vanished with its crew and passengers the white witches, and the children of the future. And so, the prophy was for filled regarding the rescue, and re homing of the white witches as they landed on Palletania and Rahattelon. So, they could begin a new life there, only a few remained on earth, who escaped at the same time as the time witches, and headed to Southern Scotland (Alba) and England in the year 200 AD. The time witches returned to

Rodicka and she filled in the gaps in the book of shadows, this made more sense in context, with the rest of the book. It also explained why, the pictures were never seen on cave walls later in history, as if they never existed.

QUEST FOR BLOOD

It was a cold winter in England of 1643 AD, the snow was thick on the ground, and the Castle was almost in darkness, the hungry wolves were prowling in the forest, and owls sat on branches in the trees, it was minus two centigrade, an icy cold night, with a full moon in the sky. The only sign of life in the castle, were bats flying around, in flocks of eight or nine. A young girl who seemed to be lost, entered the castle, she had long hair and brown eyes, wearing a skirt and blouse. Her blouse was grey and a faded, her skirt was black with flowers on. She walked down the corridors with a burning torch, which flicked in the breeze, in this draughty corridor. She appeared to be approximately sixteen years old, a with brown tanned complexion and obviously poor, perhaps a gypsy. It was unclear what she was actually doing there, but she appeared nervous and apprehensive, walking up some stone winding steps to the next level. Suddenly, she stopped as she heard footsteps, behind her, her eyes widened and she began to stare, at a shadow on the stairs.

She continued up the stair, and entered a large room, she was looking for a place to hide. She hung her flaming torch on a metal holder on the wall, and hid in an empty cupboard, and listened for sounds. She could hear the sound of footsteps getting louder and louder, until they were so close, that she could hear breathing. She could feel her heart pounding, and she knew that one single sound could give her away. Seconds went by and then a clicking sound and the cupboard door opened wide, revealing a tall dark figure. He had long dark hair, clean shaven and a dark suit with a black cape.

"Who might you be?" he asked.

"I am Margarita," she said, nervously.

"I am Lazarus," he said. "What are you doing here?"

"I am searching for my brother," she replied.

"My master Count Vermont will know," Lazarus said. "We can see him now."

"I don't want to wake him, its late." she said, trying to walk away.

"The master is nocturnal; he will be awake," Lazarus insisted.

"Still, I should go home, my mother and friends," she said backing away from him.

He stared at her his eye were red and strange, making her feel odd, she fell back onto a chair and Lazarus looked at her naked neck. He opened his mouth and fanks appeared, he edged forward to sink his fangs into her neck. Lazarus sank his fangs into her neck and proceeded to suck her blood, until she was lifeless and completely drained.

The time witches had left Rodicka, and were travelling to Aspera to see Crystal, when they were driven off course by a meteor storm, somehow the coordinates changed, and they were misdirected to Delus. They arrived close to the forest, not far from the castle, after a rough flight they managed to land safely near a desert, thanks to Maya who piloted the ship and Luna who navigated. They looked at the weather conditions, temperature and atmosphere, in order to feel safe and secure, and then they checked for life forms. Foster gave them the planets history, providing them with anything unusual, but vampires did not show up on their instruments. So, they did not exist, or they thought it maybe before they existed on Janus, after all, they had originated on earth, and travelled through the time portals.

The time witches explored the castle, walking down passageways and up spiral stairways. The lights on their headbands lit the way for them, they walked through cob webs and touched damp walls. Until they arrived in a room, they had disturbed two women with a child, by now they were using their wands for extra light. The girl seemed frightened, she was curled up in a ball, hiding her face.

"Don't be afraid," Alicia said touching her shoulder. "We are your friends."

"We are time witches," Maya said. "We want to help you."

"So, you are not vampires?" Siena asked.

"No, white witches, we help people," Luna explained. "You are in safe hands."

Elizabetha and Elena two the two vampires that had got Siena in the room were listening outside.

"They are witches, very dangerous," Elizabetha said. "One drop of their blood could kill us."

"It is said that their blood is like acid to us," Elena said. "It can strip the very flesh from us."

"Let us return to the master and tell him," Elizabetha commented.

"It's a pity," Elena said. "Such pure blood that girl has."

The time witches took Siena back to the ship, and gave her clean clothes and food. During her stay, she managed to use the shower and got to know the witches. Siena explained who she was and about the vampires.

"My name is Siena and not Sienna, I was named after the place in Italy where my grandparents come from spelt differently," Siena explained. "My mother is called Elizabeth and my father John Stapleton, but my father is known by his friends as John Stokes the famous vampire slayer. I also have a sister called Catherine, she is sweet and quiet, no trouble, not like me, I am more rebellious. The vampires have nearly got me a few times, but I always get away, somehow. I followed my father once to see why he kept going out at night, we knew nothing about what he did, it was like another life. But when I followed him, I knew he was talking to the other slayers, leading them to kill vampires."

"That must have been scary," Alicia said.

"It was every time," Siena admitted.

"I have something for you," Maya said. "It's an enchanted necklace, attached is a pearl in a tear, you need to wear it, and then whenever you're alone in danger, squeeze the tear and you will be somewhere else, safe and sound."

"Thank you," Siena said politely. "This will stay around my neck."

Siena travelled that night hoping to find her father, in the woods or castle, feeling at the enchanted necklace around her neck. the snow was thick on the ground, and the Castle was in darkness, the hungry wolves were prowling in the forest, and owls sat on branches in the trees, it was minus three centigrade, an icy cold night, with a full moon in the sky. The only sign of life in the castle, were bats flying around, in flocks of eight or nine. A young girl who seemed to be lost, entered the castle, she had long hair and brown eyes, wearing a skirt and blouse. Her blouse was white with lace and a faint sign of a pattern, as if it had faded, her skirt was dark green with flowers on. She walked down the corridors with a burning torch, which flicked in the breeze in this draughty corridor. She appeared to be approximately fourteen years old, with pale complexion and obviously poor. It was unclear what she was actually doing there, but she appeared nervous and apprehensive, walking up some stone winding steps to the next level. Suddenly she stopped as she heard footsteps, behind her, her eyes widened and she began to stare, at a shadow on the stairs.

She continued up the stair, and entered a large room, she was looking for a place to hide. She hung her flaming torch on a metal holder on the wall, and hid in an empty cupboard, and listened for sounds. She could hear the sound of footsteps getting louder and louder, until they were so close, that she could hear breathing. She could feel her heart pounding, and she knew that one single sound could give her away. Seconds went by and then a clicking sound and the cupboard door opened wide, revealing a tall dark figure. He had long dark hair, clean shaven and a dark suit with a black cape.

"Who might you be?" he asked.

"I am Siena," she said nervously.

"I am Lazarus," he said. "What are you doing here?"

"I am searching for my father John," she replied.

"My master Count Vermont will know," Lazarus said. "We can see him now."

"I don't want to wake him, its late," she said, trying to walk away.

"The master is nocturnal; he will be awake," Lazarus insisted.

"Still, I should go home, my mother will be worried," she said backing away from him.

He stared at her his eye were red and strange, making her feel odd, she fell back onto a chair and Lazarus looked at her naked neck. He opened his mouth and fanks appeared, he edged forward to sink his fangs into her neck. The last thing she did was to clutch hold of her necklace, and then all faded as she disappeared.

Siena woke up in another environment, the room was surrounded by pictures, when she felt able, she got up from the floor, and looked at them one by one. Eventually she was able to see clearly and examined one of the pictures, it seemed as if it were three dimensional, the painting of a deer. The deer appeared to stand out on the picture, as if it was in the room, looking at her. She tried to touch it, suddenly, her hand vanished in the picture, and so she pulled it out quickly, moments later she did it again sending her arm through. Eventually, she pushed her whole body through this large painting. She vanished into it, and found herself in darkness for a short time, appearing into another room. She walked out of the room, and down a flight of stairs, walking carefully because she was in semi darkness. She noticed a large door and made her exit, she expected to walk onto a snowy ground, but found her bare feet touching an unusual surface, which was sand.

She was bewildered, she had entered the castle, treading on snow, and now she was on sand, was she in a dream. It was at that moment that she saw bats, flying around her head, coming up close to her. Suddenly the changed into women, and stood in front of her, blocking her way.

"Are you going somewhere, pretty one?" one of them said.

"I think she is, Celeste," said the other woman.

"I think she wants to play, Lenora," Celeste replied.

"Please, I am lost," Siena said.

"Aww, she is lost," Lenora said. "We can help her can't we, Celeste?"

"Of course, we can, Lenora," Celeste replied. "After all she is all alone."

"Yes, and she could get hurt," Lenora commented.

Siena remembered this experience later, when she was walking in the snow to the castle, and when Lazarus had trapped her in that room, she escaped by squeezing the tear. And then again, when Celeste and Lenora had stopped her outside the castle. She was grateful to the time witches for their help, and thought of them whenever, she looked at the necklace.

The time witches continued to explore the castle, they often thought of Siena and the enchanted necklace, hoping that it would prove useful.

Elizabeth and Elena went to see count Vermont, heading through a picture/time portal back in time to the 17th century, on earth.

Vermont was stood by a picture, and saw them arrive through a painting.

"Master," Elizabetha said. "We have just seen witches at the castle on Janus."

"We had a child called Siena to bring to you," Elena said. "But they came with glowing wands."

"Foolish girls, why didn't you kill the witches," Vermont said angrily.

"They are powerful," Elizabetha said and Elena nodded in agreement.

"Nonsense," Vermont said shaking his head. "Be gone, I will send others to get them, and as for Siena, Emma and Lara will get her."

Vermont turned to two of his most trusted vampires, Cassius and Orpheus, for help.

"Cassius, Orpheus I need you to take care of the witches on Janus, Emma and Lara find Siena, search every town and village for her."

Siena had gone through another picture hoping to return home, after meeting the time witches she had returned to the earth, entered the castle out of the snow, met Lazarus, escaped with the use of the enchanted necklace, escaped from vampire women using the same method, and now she had to return home.

When Siena got home, she entered the house as if she had never left, in fact she had reached her house, earlier than when she has had left. Her mother had just cooked a meal, a beef stew which she turned down last time, but this time she had it. Her father was home, and her sister was in the room that they shared. Their mother called Catherine for tea, and they were all sat around the table, their father said a prayer, and they all ate their food.

Catherine noticed Siena's necklace, and felt compelled to comment.

"My word Siena, what a lovely necklace," Catherine commented.

"Yes, its nice," her mother agreed.

"Where did you get that?" her father asked.

"From a friend," Siena answered hoping that that was the end of the conversation.

"It looks expensive," Her mother said.

"Not really," she said sheepishly.

"I hope you haven't stolen it," her father said making her choke.

"John really," Elizabeth scolded. "As if Siena would do a thing like that."

John reached across to touch it, and Siena reacted.

"Don't touch it," she said, hysterically. "You will break it."

"Why my dear, why are you getting upset like that?" Her mother asked.

"I don't want to talk about it," Siena said, she excused herself, and went to her room.

Catherine followed her to their room; she was eager to know about the necklace and why she got so upset. Siena was looking at it through the mirror, admiring it and the way it shone in the candle light.

"It is beautiful, Siena," Catherine said. "Who got it for you?"

"Not you too," Siena said. "Why is everyone on to me."

"Oh Siena, I am your sister," she said. "You can trust me."

"Okay, but don't tell mother or father," Siena warned her. "It's an enchanted neckless, from some witches I met, it has saved my life. I almost got killed by vampires, this saved me, it transported me somewhere else. The witches saved me from the vampires too, I was lucky that they were there, all four of them.

"Real witches?" Catherine asked in disbelief. "Dark witches with broomsticks and wands."

"They were a bit different," Siena explained. "They had green outfits on and 'T' 'W' on their costumes, meaning time witches."

"Are you serious?" Catherine said. "Or is this a joke."

"No, they are white witches from the future," Siena said sincerely.

Catherine left the room, and within an hour her father entered the room, he was very upset and stood over Siena with anger in his eyes.

"Siena, what is this about witches?" he said furiously.

"She told you?" Siena said, disappointed with her sister.

"Now, take that neckless off and give it to me," he insisted.

"No, you can't have it," she replied holding on to it, trying not to press it.

But Siena knew that he wouldn't let her keep it, and eventually she handed him the necklace, and then laid down and put her head on the pillow and wept.

That evening she was being watched by her mother when her father left with his fellow vampire slayers, but when her and

Catherine went to sleep, Siena went out. She had searched for the necklace, but never found it, in the house. She headed for the woods feeling vulnerable without her necklace, upset with her sister for telling her parents.

She heard all sorts of sounds around her and thought that her father must have been there, somewhere, and perhaps hunting down vampires. She wanted to please him, and thought if she caught up with him, that she could help him. He had to understand her and her intentions, perhaps the necklace would protect him. As she got deeper into the woods, she heard owls and it was getting misty, she thought that she saw shadows, ghosts or spirits and the sound of howling wolves. She had begun to regret going on into the petrified forest, all alone without the necklace, having no protection. She was hoping that the time witches would be close by and rescue her, but they had problems of their own on Janus. Suddenly two ladies appeared in dark clothing, they stood beside Siena and began to speak softly.

"What is a beautiful girl doing here in the forest?" one of them said.

"Why Emma, I think she is lost," said the other lady.

"Lara, I do think you are right," Emma said.

"We can bring her home," Lara replied.

"Come girl, let us help you," Emma offered.

Siena searched around her neck for her necklace, and then remembered that it was missing, and so she went with the women. They took her to the castle, leading her up the stairs, Siena had been hypnotised, and was unsure exactly what was happening. On arrival into a room, Emma bit her neck and took some of her blood, Siena was already pale, became worse, almost white. She lay resting on the bed, Emma returned with count Vermont, and they were both watching her.

"Soon she will be one of us," Vermont said.

"A vampire bride," Emma replied.

"You have done well, Emma," Vermont commented.

"We are here to serve you master," she replied.

The time witches were in the castle on Janus, when the vampires went to find them. They came out of pictures and searched the castle, travelling down every corridor and rooms, even the dungeons. Eventually they found them in the main hall, they were expecting company and greeted them.

"Hello vampires, we are the time witches," Maya said.

"You have entered the castle of Janus, we are the vampires of the castle," Cassius said in reply. "You have trespassed on our property, and we will destroy you all."

"That's not very sociable," Jessica said. "In fact, it's very rude."

"Very rude," Alicia added.

"Prepare to die, witches," Orpheus said, angrily.

They began flying around the time witches, in great numbers, swirling around them. The witches created a canopy, in a design like their logo, that covered all of them. This protected them from above, while they used their wands, to protect the rest of them.

The vampires moved in to attack, each of the witches used lightning, to defend themselves, Ergokensis, and then made use of the furniture and other objects to use as missiles, known as psychokinesis. Maya added fire to her attack or pyrokinesis, causing havoc, making the vampires retreat.

"We told them," Alicia commented. "Yay, victory."

"It's not over yet," Maya said. "Do you remember what Shanice told us about the vampires?"

"Didn't they wear armour?" Jessica asked.

"Protective suits and the slayers," Maya replied. "The vampires were able to go out in daylight, they could also abduct people for harvesting, from other worlds through the time portals."

"So, they will be back," Jessica said, nervously.

"We must get the armour that Crystal was given, it will be in the ship with the weapons." Maya said, "We can also send a message to Carina, the vampire slayer."

The time witches returned to the ship, they found the contact details for Carina, and sent a message to her, at this point in time, it happened to be a little way into the future for them, so they had met the original time witches. They soon replied, and suggested that the new generation time witches suit up for action. The suits had been stored away, so they took them out and tried them on, they were surprisingly comfortable. Their necks were protected by a metal brace, secured by a strong helmet and visor, the chest armour was re-enforced to protect the heart. They set out again, heading for the castle, unaware that the vampires were in various locations of the castle, in order to catch them out. They suddenly came swooping down as bats, and transformed back into human form. They were wearing armour, and carried weapons in their hands. Their faces were covered by visors that lifted up, so they could bite their victims, they had recently abducted humans from various places in time, and they were harvesting them for blood.

The time witches sensed their presence, and braced themselves for battle, but the vampires were cunning, they tried to pick the time witches off one by one.

Alicia was the lightest, and so they picked her up first, trying to fly off with her. But she kicked one of them off, and sent the other flying into a wall, she then came down slowly to the ground. The vampire leader was Darius Larick, known to Carina, who had fought with him on numerous occasions, one of the evillest vampires.

Meanwhile on earth in the seventeenth century, Siena was trying to come to terms, with her transformation as a vampire. She had befriended a vampire bride called Ballari, a dark-haired girl, very attractive, with green eyes wearing gothic clothes. She wore a black dress with red ribbons on it, she wore dark make up, and black trousers. Siena but similar clothes on, trying to be like Ballari. They both went searching for victims, Ballari showed Siena how to hunt, and drain blood in order to survive. Siena regrated going out on that fateful night searching for her father, she was now a vampire and dependent on blood to survive. She could not go out in the daylight, or she would simply disintegrate. She was unable to visit her family again, and live in the household, she knew that was impossible. She was forced to live in this dull castle, like a prisoner in her own body, frightened to go outside in case the vampire slayers got her.

On Janus, the time witches continue to fight the vampires, trying to use the weapons that were given to their predecessors, and their own powers. But the vampires were many and greatly outnumbered them, they were becoming weaker and less able to fight them off.

Suddenly, the vampires captured them, and put them in the dungeon, in the lower level of the castle, in with those who had been abducted. During their stay, the prisoners explained to the time witches, how they were abducted, from various locations in time and space. Some were clothes shopping, and taken from changing booths, dragged into the wall, which was a time portal. Others were taken from toilet cubicles, hospitals, alley ways, lift shafts and swimming baths, wherever there was a time portal. Alicia was very chatty, and able to extract information from anyone, therefore she did most of the talking.

"Are you going to be killed?" one woman asked her. "They take your blood from you, bite your neck and drain you."

"Oh, we are not on the menu," Alicia replied. "Contaminated blood."

"What will happen to you?" she asked.

"We will no doubt be killed," Alicia said calmly.

"They call our deaths as the great feast," she explained. "We are taken to the great hall, and offered to the vampires, Darius told us."

"I am Alicia," she said, introducing herself. "This is my sister Jessica with friends Maya and Luna," she didn't mention that they were witches.

"I am Freda," she replied.

After a lengthy conversation, Alicia had learned a lot about, where they were all from, and how they got there. But the most amazing story was about using pictures for time portals, it seemed popular, and such a novel way to travel. Apparently, it was discovered by accident by a small girl called Lilly, who somehow stumbled upon it. She travelled constantly in these portals, until she became sick, due to its effect on her body. Known as Temporal displacement, which lead to pressure and eventually subarachnoid haemorrhage, and she died. It was very sad but part of the risk of time travelling through these portals, each trip was risky, and she had done it for years. Unfortunately, her discovery proved to present problems, it allowed other creatures to enter the time portals such as vampires, using them to transport their victims to another world.

Back on earth in the seventeenth century, during the English civil war, the vampire slayers were having their own war, against the vampires. The slayers had swept the forest for vampires, Emma and Lara narrowly escaped, but Siena faced her father alone.

"Father," Siena shouted without thinking.

John turned to face her, he could see that she looked different, her eyes were yellow, and as she spoke, he could see her fangs.

"What has happened to you, my child?" he asked.

"Count Vermont has battened me; I am a vampire," she said sadly.

"Then you must get away fast, before anyone sees you," he replied desperately.

"I love you, father," she said.

"Please go," he insisted.

Ballari swooped down, and took her away in the sky, Siena looked back and then flew away. The vampire slayers rushed over to John, concerned about his health, having caught a glimpse of the vampires flying away.

"Are you well, John."

"Yes, will, I am fine," he said. "I think I scared them away." John returned home to his wife Elizabeth, and his daughter Catherine, he had brought home bad news, regarding Siena.

"I saw her Elizabeth," he said, in a trembling voice.

"Who?" she asked but she had already guessed. "Siena?"

"Yes Siena," he sat down clutching his head. "She is a vampire; my own daughter is a vampire."

"Are you sure?" she asked him.

"Yes, she even looked like one, those eyes and teeth, make no mistake, she is one," John broke down and cried. "Do I have to hunt down my own daughter?"

"No, you can't," Catherine shouted from across the room. "She has been going out to find you at night, she wanted to be with you."

"But she's a vampire now," Elizabeth said. "No longer Siena, we have lost her."

"Is there nothing we can do?" Catherine asked.

"Only pray for her soul," John replied.

The time witches remained in the dungeons, they had been informed about so much, particularly about the vampires. Now they were more prepared to fight the vampires, especially as the vampire slayers were not far away. They felt that they could prevent more deaths of humans, by freeing themselves and the captives. Luna detected the slayers presence, seeing them in a vision, they were wearing the armour and carried weapons, and were coming in many numbers, led by Carina and Gareth.

Firstly, the time witches made themselves invisible, the guards were bewildered where they had gone, searching the dungeons. But as the guards entered the dungeon, the time witches left, walking up the stone stairs, stepping quietly as they went. As they reached the next level, they noticed a door leading to a room, but no one was there. They walked across the room to another door, this time they heard voices, they opened the door a crack and looked in. Lazarus and Darius were there talking, and they could see their armour in the room, but needed to distract the vampire's. Jessica made a knocking sound at another door, causing the vampires to go and investigate. During this time the time witches rescued their armour, and weapons from the room, and went back into the other room. Just as they got changed, the vampires came back from the dungeons with half a dozen prisoners including Freda. Evidently these were the next feast, towards the vampires lust for blood, which had to be stopped.

"Stop!" Maya said. "Let them go."

"Never," said the vampires who couldn't see the witches faces, hidden under helmets.

"Then suffer the consequences of our Roth," Jessica said boldly.

The vampires came nearer to the witches, each one brandishing weapons, and abandoning the prisoners, in the corner of the room. The witches had regained their energy and used their powers effectively. Alicia was using a special sword, which converted into a type of laser sword, and cut the vampires down. Lazarus had returned to the room, he heard shouting and instantly intervened. Lazarus had his own sword and battled against her, he was also wearing armour, using his sword with great skill. Alicia was also skilful with the sword, she managed to defend herself well, clashing her sword against his, until finally she beat him, plunging her sword into his chest. He fell to the ground and then rose up, grabbing her shoulder, trying to bite her neck.

"Do you want to die?" Alicia asked.

He hesitated for a moment, "Die?" Lazarus said.

"I am a witch," she admitted.

"A witch," Freda said in astonishment. "Are you all witches?"

"Yes," Jessica said. "We are all witches."

Lazarus managed to grab his sword, while everybody's attention was on the witches, and then he charged at Alicia, she jumped back and Maya shot a stake through his heart, from a cross bow, causing him to disintegrate in ashes. Before he was hit, he managed to wound Freda in the stomach, she had been standing behind Alicia. Luna dealt with her wound, using potions, before long Freda was able to stand up, trying to walk.

Maya and Jessica went to rescue the prisoners in the dungeons, and brought them upstairs with the others, once they were all together, the time witches went to check if it was safe for them to leave. They looked around outside the room and then entered the main corridor leading to the grand hallway and ballroom. There inside were the vampires battling the Carina and the slayers, using their weapons to destroy the vampires. It was quite a battle, the time witches joined them, and it was soon over. A lot of the vampires got away, though pictures, but at least a percentage of them had been killed.

On earth in the seventeenth century, John Stokes and his vampire slayers, were attacking the castle, they entered by travelling over the draw bridge, and some found a different route through a secret passage. They found the vampires and charged at them, destroying them with wooden stakes, stamping them down, some of the vampire retreated, including count Vermont, but not before he killed John Stokes, by stabbing him with a sword. Luther and Drake helped Vermont escape, before they were struck down, other vampires died with them, all turned to ashes. Once everybody had left the hall, Siena and Ballari returned, and saw the dead slayers lying around, waiting to be taken home. Siena searched for her father, who was close to a painting of a lion.

"Father," she said, with tears in her eyes. "Please, forgive me."

He opened his eyes, and looked at her. "Siena," he said in a weak voice, "My Siena, what have they done to you?"

"I could not stop them," she said. "Please understand, I love you."

"Oh Siena," he said. "I love you," he said and passed peacefully away.

The time witches were still on Janus, in the castle talking to Carina, and sorting out the humans, who had to go home, a great number of them, were taken safely through the time portals, others would be taken back to their planets by the slayers. The time witches went to find Siena on earth, they discovered her with her father's body. She didn't want to leave, and clung hold of her father, hoping for a miracle. She even appeared to be praying, pleading to God to help her, feeling helpless.

Alicia knelt down beside her, trying to comfort her, feeling her pain.

"I am so sorry, Siena," she said.

"Siena, you must go, before the slayers come for you," Maya advised.

"Do you think God can help me? Siena asked.

"Maybe he will," Luna said. "Have Faith, Faith will set you free."

Luna didn't mean it literally, that the angel Faith would set her free, she meant have hope and faith, believing in God. However, she did plant a seed, that stayed with Siena, which eventually came to grow, and she was liberated four years later.

Ballari came back to her, she was anxious to escape, and encouraged her to go with her.

"Come on Siena, we have to get away," she said concerned.

"Have you got the necklace?" Alicia asked.

"I think my father has it," Siena said searching his pockets.

"Keep it safe," Luna said. "And you be safe."

Siena found the necklace, she held onto Ballari, and squeezed the neckless and vanished.

The time witches returned to Janus, they came out of the castle and entered the ship, once they had settled down and discussed Siena, they set course for their next adventure.

DO MONSTERS REALLY EXIST

It was a dark and lonely place, that a young girl found herself in, dark, gloomy and damp. A place with endless corridors, like an old castle, a place underground, that seemed so deserted and neglected, with cobwebs everywhere. The girl seemed scared and alone, frightened, hungry, and completely lost, just feeling her way down the corridors. She was paddling in water, which was a few inches deep, listening for sounds and looking out for a light at the end of the tunnel. Finally, one occurred in the distance, shining down the corridor, lighting up her way and giving her hope to carry on. Suddenly, she heard a roar coming from behind her, and the sound of heavy footsteps, she was no longer alone.

The roaring was louder, and the footsteps nearer, she tried to run, but she was too weak, and fell to the ground onto her knees, onto the wet ground. By now the roaring sound was right behind her, so she turned around to see a large mouth that was salivating, and sharp pointed teeth that were ready to bite her. She was going to be devoured and she had no way to protect herself, and so she just screamed and screamed.

Natasha the time witch, and her husband Doran, were just relaxing on a settee when they heard the sound of screaming. Both of them responded by racing into the children's bedroom in the next room, their older child aged ten and woken from her sleep.

"Whatever is the matter, Beth?" Natasha asked her.

"Monsters!" she shouted.

Natasha comforted her, while Daren checked on her sister in the next bed, Natalie her sister was half awake, having been disturbed by her sisters screaming.

Bethany described in detail, what she had experienced, giving graphic details about the monster, she was shaking and her voice quivered as she spoke. Natalie was now fully awake and listened intently, as Bethany described the place, with the strange corridors.

"I know that place," Doran said.

"Where is it?" Natasha asked.

"Close to here," he replied.

After Bethany had calmed down, Natasha went to get her, and her sister a drink of hot chocolate, from the kitchen. On her return Bethany asked her a question, that she found difficult to answer, the type of question you dread hearing.

"Do monsters really exist?" Bethany asked.

Natasha hesitated, she knew the answer, after all as a time witch she had faced monsters, vampires, androids and all manner of things. But should she be telling her, would this make her nightmares worse, and where had she seen monsters? Many things drifted through her head, but nothing that would help Bethany, with her nightmares.

"Monster are out there, in various forms, magic can defeat them," Natasha explained.

"What is magic?" Natalie asked.

Bethany was ten and Natalie was eight, Natasha was going to teach them about magic, but she felt they were so young, and didn't appear to have developed any magical powers so far. However, that isn't to say, they hadn't got the skills, but they were developing. Most children who are from magical parents, don't develop until they are teenagers.

Or as Natasha calls them teenragers, she developed early as her hormones were changing, and puberty kicked in, showing its ugly head. She had levitated at the age of eleven, used extra sensory perception (ESP) and managed to move objects across a room. The next day, the subject for her children's home schooling was E.S.P, this was demonstrated just how far the girls had developed, and then explain their powers to them.

The next day Natasha set up the classroom for the day, she studied the curriculum, according to the federation schooling program, and added E.S.P to the program's timetable. Having set everything up, Natasha introduced them to E.S.P, it was a gradual process, that took time to plan, she had to organise it properly. Most of the federation subjects were sent to her, from the space federation headquarters. They sent film footage, science projects, history of planets, universal languages, and technical science, amongst the subjects. There were lectures and fitness instruction, as well as get togethers at the headquarters for sports events, it was a type of preschool for would be witches, warlocks and wizards. Daron was also very sporty, and taught the girls useful sports pursuits, like swimming, gymnastics and long distant running. Crystal taught them tennis, dodge ball and net ball, they referred to her as aunty Crystal, and stayed with her on her planet Aspera some weekends. Crystal was due to appear there in the next few days, the children were excited about that, and liked to hear her stories about the adventures of time witch. Natasha thought that the girls had heard about, the monsters from her stories, but Natalie was surprised when Bethany mentioned monsters, as if she didn't know what she was talking about. She may have seen something on television, or heard adventure stories from library books, but she never mentioned it.

One of the E.S.P tests was Natasha, holding up a card, and seeing if one of them could say, what was on it like a picture symbol or a number. Both told her what she needed to know, scoring 90% correctly, they even described the images. Sixth sense or psychic ability can appear in many forms, and the abilities or powers can vary from person to person, as in the cave dwellers back in history. They were all exposed to, so called harmful rays, an incredible energy, but survived having great powers but it varied from person to person.

The use or abuse of these powers, varied too as the cave dwellers divided into two separate tribes, the white witches using their powers for good, while the dark witches abused their powers for evil. The white witches like Bethany and Natalie are brought up to do good, respect others and use their powers wisely. The girls were just learning about their powers and why they had them, also, how to use them effectively. They had tried levitation, by lifting their bodies in the air and rotating themselves horizontally, also known as transvection. Psychokinesis or telekinesis moving objects without touching them, using the power of the mind. Ergokinesis, moving energy like electricity without direct interaction. Prophecy, premonition, predicting the future, which Bethany discovered that she was able to do in her dreams. Natalie was a future healer, she had what was known as energy medicine, she did this by touch mainly.

Not far from their home the craft that had crashed, was sunken down in the ground, around the immediate area was large footprints that led to the home. The footsteps vanished by a tree, close to a tunnel, going to the foundations of the house. When the dark witches destroyed the original place, the only part left was the lower part of the house. Doran rebuilt the place, modelling it off the old house, or castle, but never ventured into the cellar. However, since the crash, creatures did live down there, as Bethany saw in her nightmare, with lots of corridors, this is where Merek had his dungeons too, as Shanice was aware of when she was kept prisoner. Natasha and Doran knew of the dungeons, but never thought of the underground tunnels. The creatures hunted in the forest, eating large animals mainly, but other people also lived on Zena, and some of them became food.

Natasha and Doran prepared a meal for the family, they all sat at a table together, discussing the girls home schooling, and what work was needed for forth coming tests.

Bethany was moving table objects with her mind, sending them to her father, Natalie tried, but she couldn't quite manage to do it, so she opened her hand spread her fingers wide and tried again.

"Don't worry Nat, you will get the hang of it," Natasha said.

"Patience," Doran said. "It will work eventually; telekinesis is a funny thing."

"Why can Beth do it?" Natalie asked.

"Lifting bigger objects is harder, she can't do that yet," Doran replied.

"It takes time and patience," Natasha explained. "Like all psychic abilities."

They were disturbed by a strange sound, coming from outside, when they looked out through a window, they noticed a green mist in the sky. After a short while, each of them complained about not feel well, and started hallucinating, each of them senses were disturbed. They were seeing strange things, hearing odd sounds, they had a bitter taste in their mouths, they felt something crawling on their arms and legs, and began scratching themselves. The visual hallucinations were getting worse, or so they thought, as strange creatures entered the room. They all started running into the hallway, Natasha picked up wands for each of them, from a shelf near the stairs. They ran down a corridor, and thought that it was best, to go a through doorway, down to the cellar. Little knowing about the dangers below them, but they were being watched by unexpected squatters, the monsters that had survived the crash. They proceeded down dark corridors, Bethany began to recognise them from her nightmares, the water on the floor and cobwebs. Natasha showed the girls, how to use the wands as torches, in order to light the way ahead. As they travelled along, they all heard a roaring sound, and heavy footsteps, as Bethany described.

"This is real," Bethany said. "I am not dreaming."

"It is real," Natasha said. "Stay close."

"Speed up ladies," Doran said. "They are getting closer."

"My legs are tired," Natalie said, complaining.

Suddenly, both Natasha and Doran were pushed to the ground, by a large hand, Bethany panicked and ran holding Natalie's hand, she ran so fast that Natalie fell over. Bethany knelt down to find her sister, as she helped her up, she felt breath on the back of her neck, followed by a loud roar. Both of them screamed, then Bethany thought of her powers, and stretched out her hands, and concentrated on using her powers. With one great effort, she shouted, and sent the monster back down the corridor.

The monster lifted up and went swiftly down the corridor, there was a bright light, and the monster yelled out in pain. Both Natasha and Doran, had destroyed it with their powers, with a flash of lightning from Natasha, and fire from Doran. The girls waited for their parents to catch up with them, and then they continued down the corridor. They faced more creatures further towards the dungeons, and dealt with them similarly, until they reach a way outside. It was the same place that, the monsters had entered the building, their footprints had remained in the dirt, that was leading to the crashed ship.

The time witches had arrived, landing close to the building, and not far from the crashed ship. They entered the building through the main entrance, looking for Natasha, they all started looking around, hoping to find a clue as to where they had gone. During which time, they encountered monsters, and began fighting them. Bula Seraph appeared and joined in with his army, the Lamians, Strania and Shimick were fighting too. The time witches were trying to get rid of the harmful green mist, Luna had devised a formular to clear it, and created an antidote to protect them from harm. Natasha went aboard the time witches ship, Foster had the formular ready to go, he handed it to Natasha, and she

Returned to the building, leaving Bethany and Natalie safely in the ship. They went through the main entrance, searching each room until they discovered them fighting monsters, Lamians and Bula. Bula was getting tense, he was unable to defeat the time witches, despite the green gas, in fact, he was getting weaker. He had tried many tricks, his cunning ways found unspeakable methods of evil. Like trying to trick them with mirrors, using smoke screens, and transforming himself into hideous beasts.

Natasha thought of a plan, she knew Bula was weakening, and so she managed to deceived him, she just needed to distract him. Meanwhile there were still monsters to fight, they seemed to be coming from all directions, Alicia and Jessica had gone to look for the Lamians, knowing that they couldn't be far away, having searched the building, they went outside. The Lamians were attempting to enter the ship, trying to find a way in, as Alicia got closer, the door opened and Bethany came out. One of the Lamians rushed past her, and grabbed Natalie, quickly Bethany responded, by pointing her wand at the Lamian and shouting 'Obliterate" causing the wand to send out a bolt of lightning towards the Lamian and he disintegrated. The force from the wand knocked her over, and she fell backwards onto the ground, meanwhile, Alicia and Jessica killed the rest of the Lamians.

Natasha and Doran were successful in capturing Bula, by tricking him into thinking he had killed everyone. As he was about to celebrate, they trapped him in a room and put special handcuffs on him, that sapped his energy. They handed him over to the new generation time witches, who planned to take him back to federation headquarters. The time witches helped to tidy up, before leaving for the federation, once they had a meal together, they plotted their next course to the space federation.

CASTLE OF THE CURSED

It was in a remote place on the planet Rembergo, a desert region, in the year 3205 in earth years, a planet with oxygen and warm weather 39c. A castle that looked like a type of French design, a little like the Bastille, it was a prison for galactic villains. Known in many places as the castle of the cursed, due to the clientele, and the terrible conditions in the place. Inside the castle were special rooms for special guests, VIPs of notable reputations, mass murderers, serial killers, space pirates, and rapists. They had a recent riot where a few inmates got killed and several officers injured, with other prisoners. It was a bloodbath, people even lost limbs, and one man lost an ear. It took hours for the guards to take control, using hoses and soaking them in cold water, using weapons to force them to surrender, until they weakened and calmed down. They knew that they couldn't win, but they tried anyway, they wanted better food and better conditions. They described it as, the worst experience of their lives, and the worst conditions known throughout the universe, including earths dark history.

The time witches were sent with a new prisoner, Bula Seraph, minus his powers, he was to serve time here in Rembergo prison, for universal crimes against humanity, without parole or time out for good behaviour. Commander Shepherd had ordered his imprisonment, and he wanted the time witches to escort him to Rembergo. On the way, Bula remained quiet, not even protecting about his sentence, which was unlike Bula. They were also asked to inspect the prison, and conditions there, and see if they were complying to the humanity laws.

The time witches agreed, as they were able to infiltrate the cells undetected, using their powers of invisibility, and watching the activity around them. Once Bula was securely incarcerated, they were free to relax, and take their time planning their visitation. They sat in a room, checking for cameras, or any devises that make look suspiciously, like a camera or bugging device. Otherwise, they would have to use telepathy, as a safe way to speak to each other, that usually worked, few people were gifted in this method of conversation. Perhaps some aliens within the universe, but with addition of using Scottish Gaelic, only the witches had this ability, white and dark witches.

The time witches took no chances, they decided to communicate in Scottish Gaelic, and spoke to each other telepathically. They set out a plan on who was going to inspect which area, Luna and Maya chose the female section, and the others chose the men's section, Alicia and Jessica felt that they had chosen wrongly. The male cells stunk of human sweat, various body odours were choaking up the atmosphere, causing them to feel nauseous. 'Was it worth this torture', Alicia commented, Jessica picked up her comment and replied, 'not for all the gold on Blackbeard's ship', she replied the prison conditions were bad, there was very little in the cells, nothing but hard beds, a toilet and no privacy.

The women's cells were similar, lonely hours, being observed by cameras, and given food that a dog would reject. They were let out in an exercise yard, one attached to the men's prison and one attacked to the ladies building, transexuals were kept separate. This included any other gender, according to the laws of diversity, equality and race.

Alicia sent a message to Maya stating their situation, Maya responded with her message, stating the same thing, they had all experienced similar things, reaching the conclusion that conditions were inadequate. It no wonder these prisoners were rioting, they had committed countless crimes, some of them serial killers, who were justly convicted, but no one deserves to be treated inhumanly, not even Bula Seraph. As Luna and Maya were walking through the communal section, of the female prison, communicating with each other, someone shouted.

"Bana-bhuidsichean ùine" or "Time witches," a girl shouted. They looked around, and noticed a young girl in dark clothes, everybody thought that she was hallucinating, and one of the guards hit her on the head.

"Quiet witch," he said, threatening to hit her again. The girl was Sinead, a dark witch, who knew the original time witches. She heard their voices in her mind, and responded in Scottish Gaelic, but spoke out instead of using telepathy. She repeated herself, this time as a telepathic message, hoping that they would respond to her.

"Are you Sinead?" Alicia asked her.

"Yes, I got captured by the space pirates," she explained. "They got captured by the federation, and blamed me for their piracy. Consequently, I was imprisoned and they were taken to the male prison, but they lied about me. I have done wrong in the past, but this time I am innocent, honestly, cross my heart" she said trying to convince them.

"We will speak to the governor," Maya said.

She seemed pleased with Maya's response, and stopped communicating, the guards were watching her closely, in case she spoke again.

Luna and Maya left the communal room, and went back to the main department between prisons, where Alicia and Jessica were waiting for them.

"We have seen some space pirates," Alicia said.

"We saw Sinead, the dark witch," Maya said. "Apparently wrongly arrested."

Some of the prisoners were trustees, model prisoners who through good behaviour, were allowed to have special duties and privileges. Like working in the library, and taking books to prisoners, or other useful jobs, but some were just popular with the governor.

For whatever reason, known only to him, he had the final say about prisoners and their rights, who were to be punished, and who were in favour. John Bull Bowly was his name, a larger-than-life Bully, who looked like a walrus and a lion mixed together, like one of doctor Edward Douglas freaks, he was definitely borderline personality disorder. He had an instant dislike to the time witches, he considered them, a load of interfering, female men haters, with nothing better to do than meddle with his affairs. He warned them that, if they continued to interfere, he would put them in a cell with the other women. They were naturally concerned about this, and considered him as a corrupt governor, after what he could get from the system. Of course, they had to prove that he was corrupt, find evidence of what he was up to, they had heard that, he had caused disappearances of prisoners, even deaths by suspicious circumstances.

At the space federation headquarters, Commander John Shepherd was informed of Bulls deeds, Luna and Maya had entered his office invisibly, and listened in on conversations, between him and some of the prison guards. He revealed that, he had caused the riots as a decoy or smoke screen for his other work, to form an army and steal gold from the pirates, then attack merchant spaceships and blame the pirates. He could get a strong army by his side, but he needed somebody powerful to lead them, none other than Bula Seraph a powerful wizard. The commander ordered a fleet of ships to go to Rembergo, and help the time witches stop his plan from happening, but time was running out for the time witches, who had been thrown into cells.

This time Sinead could see the young time witches, she was so relieved to have company of her own kind, as she put it. But they needed a way out, the guards were watching them, in case they were able to use their powers, all though the wrist bands they were wearing made them weak. Foster had informed, Strania and Shimick that the time witches were in danger, and so they instructed Foster to contact federal headquarters. The commander was furious with Bull, and made the order his fleet to depart immediately to Rembergo.

Meanwhile, the female prisoners were put to work, mining for gold below the surface, while the men were made, to prepare one of the ships for battle. Bula was released to meet Bull as planned, he knew what he wanted, and said that he would lead the prisoners into battle. It was obvious that Bula had planned this, and his arrest, so that he could be part of this wicked plan. Maya tried to verbally discuss her plan of escape, but the guards over heard her, and struck her across the head with a thick stick. She fell to the ground, bleeding from the forehead, Luna knelt down to help her, but she got kicked in the stomach.

The weather began to change outside, a storm was fast approaching, the prisoners were sent back to their cells. As for Bula Seraph, he was taken to the prison governor, escorted by guards, bound with the same wrist bracelets, that the time witches were wearing.

This dampened his powers, making him weak and vulnerable, but the evil wizard knew he was useful to governor Bull. And it fitted with his plan, which was to cause havoc around the galaxy, taking whatever, he wanted.

"Bula Seraph, we meet at last," Bull said greeting him.

"I have heard so much about you, Governor Bowly," Bula replied.

"Call me Bull," he said, offering him a seat.

"So, what did you want with me, Bull?" Bula asked.

"Your power and leadership," Bull replied. "In return you get freedom and a handsome reward."

"This sounds interesting," Bula said. "Freedom and a reward."

"I am glad to have you aboard," Bull said happily.

"Wait," Bula interrupted Bull. "But I want something else."

"What would that be?" Bull asked, inquisitively.

"The death of the time witches," Bula insisted. "Done discretely, like an accident at work maybe."

"It's as good as done, Bula," Bull said smiling.

Bull explained his plan to Bula, going into great detail, without missing anything.

Bula was excited, he had the choice of prisons he needed, to execute his plan, the most wicked and notorious rebels in the universe. A mixture of aliens and monsters, pirates and human crossed with animals, with various abilities, the scum of the galaxy. They all had bracelets attached to them, if they tried to remove them, they would explode. They had transmitters in them, with tracking devices, so the governor could keep track of them, at all times. The governor trusted no one, not even Bula Seraph, who was a powerful wizard, and who was known for his cunning ways. Bula used people, he got what he wanted from them, and then destroyed them, he was worse that the evil wizard Merek, who created him, and then Bula killed Merek.

The expected storm was now overhead, with winds blowing and rain beating down, the governor had planned another riot, in order to cause confusion, while the prisoners escaped with Bula. Using a spaceship to fly away, armed and ready for combat, heading for the nearest cargo ship, dressed as space pirates. The prisoners who were working, got caught up in the riot as planned, and the guards searched for the time witches, knowing they were powerless. What they did not anticipate was that, Strania and Shimick were in the prison, also looking for the time witches. They managed to enter the building during the prison escape, and sneaked through the corridors, onto the women's section of the prison, a guard that was injured, had an implement attacked to his belt, so they took it. It was chaos everywhere, with fighting and screaming everywhere, Strania saw Alicia and raced to her. Alicia recognised the implement, as a form of key for the bracelets, around their wrists, and pointed it at them pressing to operate it. Quickly they searched for the other time witches, who were caught up in the riot.

Some of the guards noticed Luna and Maya, and headed towards them with weapons, following their orders to kill them. Strania and Shimick both had laser guns, they were prepared to do battle, if necessary, in order to save the time witches. One of the guards had a long knife, he was standing behind Jessica, about to stab her in the back. Strania fired her weapon, and hit him in the head, narrowly missing Jessica, who jumped out of the way of somebody else. Shimick fired at the other guard, causing him to stumble down, and Jessica jumped over him, like a true gymnast. Strania reached Jessica, and took the bracelets off. Alicia led them to Luna and Maya, so that they could release them from their bonds, but other guards were attacking them. Alicia was determined to stop them, but she was still weak, from the effects of the bracelets, Strania and Shimick were needed again to take action. They got into position, aimed their lasers, and fired at the guards, hitting both of them, Maya got injured by the cross fire. Luna was badly bruised from being battered with sticks, she had blood on her face and hands. It took a short while to get their powers back, but eventually they escaped from the riot, and found a quiet area to rest. During this time, they had time to fully recover, Maya dealt with Luna's wounds, and her own, while Alicia looked out for prison guards.

Bull was waiting for Bula to contact him, so that he could escape before the federation fleet arrived, he knew that he might be found out, regarding his plan. He arranged a ship to take him to Bula, with a few corrupt prison guards. Then he had a call that the riots had ended, but he didn't hear from the guards, about the unfortunate accident of the time witches. Finally, he received a call from a guard, saying that they were all dead, and Bull sighed with relief, no more trouble from them he thought.

Bull prepared to leave his office, in order to board the ship, and escape from the prison. He seemed so smug, as he put a few items together in a bag, and opened the door to leave.

"Are you going somewhere, Bull?" Maya asked blocking his way.

"There is no hurry," Jessica said. "Why not stay for lunch."

"Are you all ghosts?" he said, in shock. "You are all dead."

"It's funny what a voice simulator can do," Jessica said. "It can simulate any voice, like a guard, even your pathetic voice."

"I think he needs a cell of his own," Alicia advised. "To suit a wurzel like you."

"It sounds perfect," Luna said. "What a riot."

"You can't do that, I am the prison governor, I am in charge," he protested.

"You were in charge," Maya said. "Now we are in charge, prisoner x."

He attempted to leave, but Alicia stretched out her arms, and opened out her hands, Bull began to float in the air, and then using her power, she threw him back against a wall.

"You have your powers back," he said, with surprise.

"Yes, fully restored, no thanks to you," Jessica said.

In another area of the galaxy, Bula was leading the attack of a cargo vessel, dressed as space pirates, and stealing their cargo. He was leaving messages about being a pirate, hoping that it would fool the space federation.

The federation fleet arrived at the prison, the guards were called together, and Bull was sent into a cell, in order to experience prison life. They were unable to let him out of the cell, and so he just looked out of the glass re-enforced door. The time witches conversed with the captain, and then spoke to the commander, via the monitor.

"I hear you have had it tough girls," he said.

"Yes, commander." Maya replied. "Prison life is not for me."

"Nor me," Alicia agreed. "Give me a holiday resort anytime."

"A place with a cool moonlight," Luna explained. "Home from home."

The commander laughed at Luna's remark, and then he became serious again.

"I must just say that Luna has grown up and opened up more recently," he remarked.

"Yes, that is thanks to Maya," Luna admitted. "She has been my rock."

"Well, that's good," he said, but then he paused as if he was thinking, he seemed concerned about something, and then he continued.

"I need your help ladies," he began. "I need to find Bula Seraph, he must be stopped, and the prisoners brought back."

"We can do that," Maya said.

"But it means great danger," he said concerned.

"We laugh in the face of danger," Alicia said.

"We can handle it," Jessica said. "Awesome."

The commander allowed some of the fleet to go with them, led by admiral Grey a tall and well-built officer, clean shaven with blue eyes and a prominent chin. He was a fine officer, trustworthy, honest, and sincere, with an understanding nature, firm but fair.

When it was time to go, the admiral prepared his men and women by briefing them on the mission, the time witches sat in out of respect for him. He spoke about courage and bravery, and about loyalty for the space federation, comradeship and teamwork in the face of battle. The captain of each vessel to, lead his crew by setting an example, to do what I do and what I say. After the briefing, each ship was prepared for take-off, including the time witch ship 'Gena' armed for action, and ready to go. Each one took off one by one, the last one being Gena, with the time witches, Strania, Shimick and Foster. Maya was piloting the ship, and Alicia was navigating, Foster was checking the conditions in space, While Jessica was in charge of weapons. Luna was concentrating on locating Bula, using her powers to find him, any kind of images, or signs of precognition would help. Strania and Shimick offered to help, where they might be needed, keeping them, all fed and watered.

The fleet and the time witches, arrived in the area in space, where the cargo ships were attacked, the crafts were sending distress calls. Each ship circled the crafts, and some of the crew, including the time witches went aboard. The crew were discovered locked in a large room, all but the one that made the distress call, he was left to roam and contact the

Federation for help.

Bula merely wanted to show off, letting the federation know, that the ships had been invaded by pirates. But in reality, it was him, he wanted the glory, it was Bull who thought of blaming the pirates. The time witches found evidence that it was Bula, and the escaped convicts, who had raided the ship, they could tell he had used his powers. He couldn't resist showing off, he left clues everywhere, with his individual signature, leaving his mark on some of the crew. He had burnt Bula on their backs, leaving them in agony, or sticking them against a wall, by melting them to the metal. Some of the female prisoners, had scratched some of the crew, down their faces with their sharp nails.

The time witches had an idea, which was to use a cargo ship, and hide inside so they could catch the prisoners. They arranged a few of the crew to stay aboard, and pilot the ship in the direction of their ship, and then take them by surprise. This resulted in Bula attacking the ship, but what they didn't expect was for Bull, to escape and warn Bula that the federation was onto them. The two guards that helped him escape, were with him in his ship, eager to join in the next attack. The cargo ship was signalled by Bula, demanding that they stop and allow them to board, but Bull neglected to mention about the time witches. Bula was convinced that they were dead, and became excited about his next raid, unaffected by anyone.

The cargo ship was boarded by Bula, Bull and the convicts, Bull stood by Bula talking about how easy it was to take the ship, little knowing that they had already raided this one. It became obvious when the cargo was missing, Bula suspected something was wrong, and ordered his men to inspect the ship.

"I a surprise guest aboard," Bula said.

"Who might that be?" asked Bull.

"Come and meet your jailer, my girl." Bula said. "Out of the crowd of prisoners came a familiar face."

"Sinead, my dark witch and friend," Bula said happily.

"I am here to serve," she said. "Whatever you wish?"

"She is powerful, and since the time witches are no more," Bula was interrupted.

"That isn't quite true," Bull said. "They are in fact alive."

"What!" Bula shouted. "That's impossible, they were killed by your guards."

"They escaped," Bull replied. "I am so sorry."

"You fool, Bull!" Bula shouted angrily and sent a lightning bolt at Bull, killing him instantly.

"Bula, we must find them and kill them ourselves," Sinead suggested. "They are ruining our plan."

"I wonder where they are now," Bula said. "They are a thorn in my side."

At that moment they all appeared, but all they could see was their silhouettes, with a light behind them, until they came forward into the corridor.

"Are you looking for us?" Maya said.

"The time witches," Bula said. "With charmed lives, who survived the castle of the cursed."

"We are now going to bring you to justice," Alicia said.

"Surrender now and face your destiny," Jessica commanded.

"Never!" Bula shouted and ordered his convicts to attack them.

Both female and male convicts raced forward, savage creatures, along with strong and fierce animal like creatures, charged towards them. The time witches were ready for them, using their powers to defeat them, trying to spare their lives. But unfortunately, the convicts continued to fight, and some did get killed, the witches used their powers to resist their attack. They fought for an hour or two, the witches used lightning, flames and sent heavy objects at the convicts, using telekinesis. Once the time witches were victorious, they gathered up the surviving convicts, and took them to the main door. By this time the federation stepped in, and took the prisoners back to Rembergo prison. As for the time witches, they went back to the space federation headquarters, to visit commander John Shepherd, as he had a special assignment for them. Bula and Sinead had escaped during the battle, but the time witches knew, that they would see them again, some day.

INQUISITIVE MINDS

On a planet called Tallafus some distance away, in another galaxy, there exists a planet, unlike earth, with a toxic atmosphere, and three moons. It had a rugged surface and hardly any water, definitely not the place for humans, but a base was there of some kind, with cylindrical shaped buildings. Inside their lived aliens, strange beings with odd bodies and large heads, pale and looking malnourished. They communicated telepathically, using their minds to converse and hand to conduct things to move with telekinesis, only touching in the cases of procreation. They had many abilities, or extra sensory perception (E.S.P) it was their way to survive, an advanced race who, survived by learning from other planets mistakes. So called civilizations like earth, with their history of violent wars, famine, cruelty and the ruining of their habitat, namely forests and the atmosphere. Or other planets like Grancarna the green planet, with their wars and devastation, so many planets in conflict, and corruption from mankind.

Tallafus was once a trading place, until criminals arrived and stole from the Tallafans, a peaceful people, since then they have, closed their doors to the universe. But they continue to explore the galaxy for life, hoping to find a race like themselves, a peaceable, caring kind, unspoilt by hatred and greed. Their inquisitive minds led them to take people from other planets in order to examine them, they didn't think of this as a crime. Although, according to galactic law, it was classed as abduction or kidnapping in some cases, if it required a ransom, or unlawful imprisonment. The Tallafans thought it was the right thing to do, in which to study humanity, and suggest improvements to a planets' inhabitant. The alien abductees were treated well, they had nice accommodations, food and a varied selection of fluids, interactive game consoles, and activity rooms.

At the space federation headquarters, the time witches were talking to commander Shepherd, discussing the last mission, and how Bula managed to escape.

"Ladies, you did well at the prison," he said, complimenting them.

"Yes, but we lost Bula Seraph," Maya admitted.

"And Sinead, the dark witch," Alicia said. "She convinced us that she was a victim."

"She was with Bula," Jessica said. "As one of his followers."

"Well now we have another problem," the commander informed them. "A planet of aliens called the Tallafans, keep taking people from other planets, to their planet called Tallafus. They are studying aliens, for what reason is unknown, but they need to know that they are breaking the galactic law. Also, a Princess from Quastara has gone missing, can you see if they know anything."

"Have the relatives got any jewellery? Luna asked. "I am able to read things off them."

"I will ask them," the commander replied.

"It's called psychometry, it come from the energy of a person," Luna explained.

"We will investigate," Maya said. "After refreshments of course."

"Of course," the commander said. "Feel free."

"That's nice to hear after prison," Alicia commented.
After lunch the time witches set off to their ship, the commander gave them some jewellery belonging to princess Sabrina, and a message from Queen Juliet, telling them that she has a scar, on the lower right side of her abdomen, from an appendectomy. A lifesaving operation years ago, that required the removal of her appendix. This was a useful description and information for purposes of identification, apart from blonde hair and green eyes, a slim girl about eighteen years old.

The time witches set course for Tallafus, this time Alicia piloted the ship, Maya navigated, Jessica helped with refreshments, and Luna went somewhere quiet to study the jewellery, using her powers of psychometry. She spent hours in silence, studying a necklace that she was drawn to, it took approximately fifteen minutes, to come up with something. After this flood of images came to her, along with dates and time periods, things relevant to Sabrina. The images were of her family, and rooms in the palace, various faces of people in the palace, she already had a picture of her, and her immediate family. She was with her mother queen Juliet, father Jason who died, Sister Sheenah and brother David. The information coming to her, was in the form of short performances, like talking to people and going places, much like a short movie. Luna had to piece it together, and make sense of it, which was difficult not knowing the princess. But she tried hard to link everything, she was curious to know the facts, as she was the most inquisitive of the time witches.

Strania joined Luna towards the end of her psychometry, and Luna asked her to try to read from it, at first Strania was reluctant, but Luna persuaded her to try.

"Relax," she said. "Concentrate on the necklace, and tell me the first thing that come to mind."

"Nothing," Strania replied. "Take your time, allow the energy to enter your mind."

"Okay," Strania said with her green flesh glowing.

Moments passed, and then Strania suddenly got excited, she was like a child with a new toy, she glowed even more, just like a green light bulb.

"My," she said with excitement. "I see a beautiful palace, with gold and white wall designs, a queen and a princess, with crowns on their heads. It disappeared, now I see two men arguing, one of them is older, and very bossy. I see blood and a dagger, it's a murder, the older man has stabbed the youth. Now I see the young princess crying, she is very sad, something is seriously wrong, she distraught. I must stop now" Strania said, looking tired.

"It can tire you out at first," Luna explained. "But you did well, you are psychic."

"Really!" Strania said surprised.

"Yes, absolutely." Luna said smiling. "That's brilliant."

"Not brilliant, awesome." Alicia said entering the room.

"Who's flying?" Luna asked.

"Chill man," Alicia said. "Jessica took over, we are about to land."

"We had better join them," Luna said. "Buckle up."

They all prepared for landing, Maya had contacted the aliens, the Tallafans, who gave them permission to land, they were curious to know why they were visiting. However, because it was a mission by the federation, it must have been important, and relevant to them in some way. The time witches were greeted by the Tallafans, using telepathy, as their form of communication, which suited the witches. They were taken on a tour of science laboratories, demonstrating tests that were being carried out on their guests, those they had abducted according to galactic law. One alien was being scanned called Tony Lincoln from earth, another was having an Xray called Velesa. Alison Mason and Gillian Dale were gowned up ready for their scans, Amelia King, Roger Edge and Palio Mandelo were talking about their home planets. Caligo was from Grancarna the green planet, the aliens were fascinated from their green skin pigment. Shimick knew Caligo from the green planet, as a school friend, Caligo said that he was walking close to the mountains when he got lifted up into the alien vessel. He was scared at first, but the aliens promised that, he would come to no harm. They kept their promise and treated him well with food and accommodation, as well as fitness activity. All they wanted to do was to study their race, by using equipment designed to, check their organs and body structure. They proved to the witches than, no procedure posed as a risk to anyone.

Everybody was safe and returned them to their own planet, having benefited from their experience. The main important thing was that, their medical knowledge was advanced, compared to other planet, and they were able to cure people of many diseases, including cancer. The just needed to know that, they could not abduct people, from other planets, there was a way to find patients, without breaking the law. It was suggested that the federation helped, get volunteers for such studies, those willing to help. Telepathy was a great way to communicate, but after a while it became, difficult for the witches to concentrate. It was such a strain on their minds, due to the amount of energy required. The time witches spent a few days on Tallafus, getting to know the guests and asking them about their experiences, with positive answers on each occasion. Miggle Massey was the leader of the Tallafans, who showed them records and results of guests, knowing that they were looking for princess Sabrina. It took a while, searching through the list until they finally discovered her, a photograph appeared of her being scanned showing her appendix scar. She had been wearing an emerald ring, but removed it while they were scanning her, the aliens passed it to them.

"She left this behind," one of them said.

"Luna and Strania can read this, using their powers of psychometry." Maya said, passing the ring to Luna.

"Yes, we will work it out," she agreed taking Strania by the hand, and leading her to a quiet place, where they could study the ring.

The emerald ring consisted of three emerald stones on a gold band, it was Sabrina's birth stone for the month of May, given to her on her eighteenth birthday, by her mother and father. Luna held it first, and started seeing images of her sister Sheenah and uncle Edward, they had plotted to abduct her. As it was, the aliens had beat them to it, and it appeared when they arrived, they were rescuing her, taking them away from the planet. Sabrina thought that she was going home, but they took her elsewhere, to another side of the same planet of Quastara, As Sheenah wanted to be the next Queen. Edward just wanted the power to rule as a prince, next to Sheenah as her right-side man, as her adviser. He was a cunning man, with evil intent, he would rule the land with an iron fist, and Sheenah would be a figure head. Edward had a deep voice, large portly stature, and a large fat nose, with a brown beard, and wearing fine clothes.

Sheenah had a smooth soft complexion, with dark hair, and always seemed to be frowning, known to be moody and jealous of princess Sabrina and prince David. Luna and Strania had gathered up information between them, once they had compiled the story of the princess, they fed back the information to others. The story was quite shocking, regarding uncle Edwards plot against the royal family, assisted by Sabrina's sister princess Sheenah. But what did they plan to do with Sabrina? And how far were they willing to go?

The time witches had spent a while with the Tallafans, and examining their work, they had convinced them to, contact the federation headquarters, if they needed volunteers in the future. They also reminded of the galactic laws on kidnapping, which they understood, and complimented them on their life saving work. Each person was provided with a tracker in their arm, in order for the aliens to track the guest's progress.

The time witches spoke to all the guests who seemed happy with stay and had freely cooperated with each test, nobody suffered any ill effects due to tests.

It was time for the witches to go, but they did get tested themselves before leaving, each one had a remarkable result, confirming their powers were fully charged to find the princess. They did promise to return in the future, but as Jessica said, "We have got to go and save the universe."

THE RING, THE CRYSTAL AND THE PRINCESS

The princess was staying at her uncle Edward's home, at a country manor on the eastern side of the planet Quastara, she considered herself a guest, at this time. She believed that she had been rescued by him, while staying at the alien planet Tallafus, although they looked after her. The feedbacks were all on digital recorders, from scans to interviews, which she saw on screen, highlighting her appendix scar on the lower right-hand side of her abdomen. She was given a copy of her tests, the monitor remained in her arm, unknown to anyone, but herself and the time witches. One day she overheard her sister talking to her uncle, about her stay, which greatly disturbed her.

"What are we going to do with her, Edward?" Sheenah asked.

"I really haven't thought yet," Edward replied.

"I thought those aliens were going to keep her," Sheenah said. "Abduct her and keep her, but they let all persons return home."

"She may have to die," Edward explained. "She knows too much already, about our plans."

"Kill her, surely not," Sheenah said, horrified.

"You want to be queen?" Edward said, struggling into a chair.

"Not that much," she said. "I don't want to harm her."

"Nonsense, you want to be queen, and me I want to be at your side as advisor," Edward said confidently. "I killed the king, so it would not take much to kill Sabrina."

"I don't like this," Sheenah said. "That's murder."

"Don't back out now, you wanted her out of the way," Edward was becoming angry.

"But I never wanted to harm her," Sheenah said upset.

"Too late, Sheenah!" he shouted. "Your sister must die!"
The time witches arrived on Quastara, they decided to land a few miles away from where the signal was coming from, telling them where Sabrina was. The object was to get inside the building undetected, so they made themselves invisible, before infiltrating the building. Not knowing the layout of the building, they all chose different directions and communicated telepathically. All searching the bedrooms, until one of them found her, they had twelve rooms to search for her. But they noticed Edward enter one of them, with Sheenah, Alicia followed her in, and stood in the corner watching them. The others stayed outside the door, waiting to be called, they

knew that Edward intended to kill the princess. Edward looked over her, and began to whisper to Sheenah, over Sabrina's head.

"She is asleep," he said. "Get that spare pillow, and push it over her face!

"I can't," she said. "Don't make me."

"Do it!" he insisted. "Or, you will die!"

"No!" she shouted, hoping to wake her sister.

Edward was furious and grabbed the pillow from her, and put it over her face. Alicia kicked him and sent him flying across the room, he thought it was Sheenah and pulled out a dagger. Jessica sent a lightning bolt towards him, causing him to fall to the ground, in pain, injured and confused. The time witches began to appear, and stopped Sheenah from leaving the room, while the princess awoke to all the commotion.

"What is happening?" she asked.

"Princess Sabrina?" Alicia asked her.

"Yes, I am Sabrina," she replied.

"Do you have a scar on the right side of your abdomen?" Jessica asked her.

"Yes, I do," she said showing her.

"We are here to take you home," Maya said. "And arrest your relatives for abduction, on behalf of the space federation and your royal family."

"This is yours," Luna said, giving her the emerald ring. "This is how we found you, and a tracker in your arm, that the aliens instilled in you."

"Thank you," she said. "You evidently saved me; I am most grateful."

They took everybody on the ship, and travelled to the palace, where everybody was waiting for them, giving Sabrina a fine reception, with a fanfare and cheering from the crowd. Queen Judith had a private conversation, with the time witches regarding Sheenah and Edward, trying to resolve the situation, or making sense of why they acted so badly.

"Your majesty" Maya said respectfully "We caught Edward and Sheenah in the room, Edward wanted Sheenah to kill the princess, by smothering her with a pillow. However, Sheenah refused to kill her sister, she just wanted capture her and become the next queen. She had no intention to hurt anyone, she was misled, and not a killer"

"Very well," she said. "She still has to be punished," she insisted.

"All we ask is leniency, your majesty," Alicia said. "After all she was misguided by Edward."

They stopped long enough to see, the outcome of Edward and Sheenah's trial, which turned out favorable for Sheenah who was charged with kidnapping, facing no jail time. Edward was charged with attempted murder, kidnapping and treason, he was sent to space prison for twenty years, without parole. Sheenah was remorseful, and from this day forward she was loyal to her sister, and they became close. Princess Sabrina wanted to talk to the time witches, about a crystal she had found, thinking it may be enchanted.

The crystal that she showed them, appeared long and the time witches discovered it had a life of its own, they had never seen one quite like it, it was unique. Although it appeared like glass, various colour's showed through it, changing all the time, like traffic lights. She gave it to Luna, so that she could examine it, upside down, from the top, in front of her eyes and then Luna sent it floating in the air.

"It is remarkable," Luna said.

"Awesome," Alicia agreed.

"I see great wonders," Luna said. "This whole palace alive with guests, celebrating a wedding, with people from all over the galaxy, so much happiness."

"You see all this," Sabrina said happily. "It is a remarkable crystal."

"Don't you see anything?" Luna asked.

"Not a thing, but many colours," she replied disappointedly.

"Look again," Luna insisted.

Sabrina took another look, this time to her surprise, she saw many things, she was so excited, everything was clear and revealing.

"Thank you, Luna," she said. "You have cleared the fog from my eyes, I can see clearly now."

"I am glad to help," Luna said. "If ever you need me, I will be around, just look into the crystal and call me."

The time witches said farewell, and went back to their ship, preparing for their next adventure, wherever that may be.

THE CHARLATANS

It was in the year 1860, in Victorian times, that the old musicals were popular, audiences would flock into theatres, and see their favorite acts live, performing on stage. There was no television, or any modern gadgets to speak of, or record players, only live stage performances. This is when the great Branzino appeared with his able-bodied assistant Maria, doing mind reading, and other illusions, but what was not known was that Branzino was from the future, and used futuristic gadgets to perform his tricks. Nothing about this couple was genuine, they were what people of today know as charlatan's. They charged people money to contact dead relatives, performed on stage tricking the audience. They used ear pieces to contact each other, vanishing boxes with tiny explosives, illuminating light effects operated by batteries, and many other devices. One box is a transporter, that takes people elsewhere, to a different universe, or time. This device was prone to go wrong, leaving people stranded, they would probably never reach home again. They were the type to play with people's emotions, providing them with cold readings about lost relatives, and sad lives based on observation of their appearance. The object was to look at a person, and see a badge about saving the earth, and say you care about the environment, or say they have a scar on their knee, which is quite common. Charlatans exist everywhere, making money from people, who have lost someone in death, or wanting good news about their future. Some could be classified as sociopaths, because they have no conscience, they just don't care who they hurt. People with genuine abilities, are frowned upon because of these charlatans, no one will listen to them, even if they get a premonition about something important, like a murder, or kidnapping.

The old-time musical began with a sing along, introduced by a compare, this was followed by a comedian, and then the great Branzino and Maria. He started his act with a few magic tricks, and then went into his medium act, talking about the dead, and pointing out random people in the audience, making out he was speaking to a dead relative. Sometimes he got a name right, or place of residency, perhaps a city or town. Studying the person and their reactions to his questions, whatever may have been useful at the time.

He was making a fortune, each night that he performed and gained followers, as a time traveler, he was able to make money with a lot of ventures, by gambling, finding rare and coins. He would study the football pools, from a certain date, and arrive a week earlier to fill in the pools and win the next week.

The time witches arrived in London, at a familiar age in Victorian England, they had been discussing extra sensory perception (E.S.P) and the advantages it had in society. Luna was very keen on this subject, having these powers as the others did, but having these from birth, and using them from an early age. The others developed their power later, with practice and having the help from family and the school of magic. Sometimes, it was frustrating, because they were advised, not to use them in public or in a non-magic environment, some magic was considered dangerous, some even banned. But dark witches used it, they didn't care who they hurt, usually white witches like Maya, Luna, Alicia or Jessica. It was getting late, and the theatres were opening, the cues were lining up down the street, people dressed in fashionable attire, Victorian outfits. Women in long dresses with plenty of lace, and tight corsets, flowers in hats, looking so elegant. Men in suits, and top hats looking dapper, or an equally smart attire.

The time witches dressed themselves up for the occasion, coping the dress for this period, each one looking so beautiful. And then they lined up, waiting to enter the theatre, eager to see this performance, that they had heard so much about. Watching the dancers, singers and comedians, and then finally Branzino, who appeared with Maria. Maria didn't seem happy, she was moody, she shouted at Branzino, and glared at him many times. Branzino seemed calm, and relaxed during his performance, but he was finding it difficult to concentrate, and slipped up sometimes. When he addressed the audience, it was as if he was in a trance, asking the usual questions like has anybody got an aunty Ethel or uncle George, and then Maria brought in the box on wheels, which looked like a cupboard or coffin. They choose someone from the audience to go inside, and shut the door, moments later he vanishes, never to be seen again. While most people clap, his wife is concerned about him, wondering where he has gone, and if she will see him again, so after the show she tries to find Branzino, but he has vanished too. In her desperation, she contacts the police, but they cannot help her, only investigate the theatre. Maya hears the lady shouting, and offers to help her find her husband, she asks her for any jewelry such as a ring or a watch, anything connected to her husband. The lady shows her a pocket watch, of her husbands, which she held on to, Maya gives it to Luna, who sits down in a theatre seat meditating, using her telekinetic skills. Meanwhile, Maya questions her, about her husband, background and personality, his hobbies and skills, trying to find a common ground.

It seemed to take a long time, gathering up information, but Maya and her friends built up a picture of the man Gilbert and his wife Janet, their home life, and his personality.

Gilbert was a kind man, very sensitive and nervous, a little shy, but clever and artistic. Janet was confident, bright, assertive and protective, she was Gilberts back bone, encouraging and offering reassurance. Maya gathered from this, that Janet wore the trousers in their relationship, Gilbert's sensitivity held him back, he was thin in stature and looked weak, Janet was a lioness, a woman who hunted for food and took care of her pride. Luna returned with the fob watch, having more answers for Janet.

"Branzino knows you," she said.

"I don't know him," she replied bluntly. "I have never met him before."

"He knows about your children?" Luna said, "Tom and Caroline."

"They are my children," she admitted. "But how did he know?"

"Because he has been watching you," Luna explained. "Obviously for a while."

Jessica and Alicia joined them, both very excited and bursting to tell Janet the news.

"We think we can get your husband back," Jessica said.

"But you must trust us," Alicia said.

"How can you do that?" Janet asked. "He vanished in a box."

"Trust us," Jessica said. "Give us time."

"Maya, we need you and Luna."

Maya and Luna walked with them to the box, and they showed them how he had been transported, from one place to another, using the box.

"This is no ordinary box; it transports objects and people from one place to another," Jessica explained.

"We need to run a trace on the destination of these people," Alicia said.

"I agree," Maya said. "We need our equipment to trace this."

"They returned to the ship, Luna gave Strania the watch and asked her to see what she might find with her telekinetic skills, while they prepared the equipment to check the inside of the box. Foster prepared the program for time travel locations and possible destinations, mapping out courses on the computer.

Jessica and Alicia returned to the theatre, and tested the box, and relayed the information back to the ships computer, each time the box was used it was recorded in a panel in the box, with time location, in order to determine the destination. With this in mind, they could locate Gilberts whereabouts, and rescue him, returning him home. It was obvious that Branzino had lost many people through this box, by meddling with something that he didn't understand, in order to fool people into thinking that he was a magician. The charlatans were exposed, but they had vanished, probably in their own time trap, lost somewhere in time.

"Jess, we have to try this out," Alicia said.

"No way," Jessica replied. "It is too risky."

"Chicken," Alicia replied. "You never want to take risks."

"You forget Alicia, I am the sensible one," Jessica said. "I don't believe in gambling with my life."

"Jess," Alicia said. "Your boring," she said closing the door.

"What have you done?" Jessica asked, "Idiot!"

"Nothing happened," Alicia said, disappiontedly.

Jessica opened the door. "Really!" she said look out here.

They were in some kind of prison, a young woman in rags was sitting on the ground surrounded by straw, the box disappeared.

"A one-way trip, obviously," Alicia said.

"Obviously," Jessica said. "What an idiot!"

"I am sorry, Jess," Alicia confessed. "I really thought it was safe."

"No problem, we are just stuck here forever," Jessica said sarcastically. "Welcome to the hotel California."

"It's a prison, Jess," Alicia explained.

"Der, I can see that," Jessica replied. "You are great at stating the obvious."

"I am really sorry, Jess," Alicia said sincerely.

"So you keep saying, but that's not going to get us out of here," Jessica said angrily.

They both looked at the poor woman opposite, in dirty clothes and long scraggily hair, that was matted, she looked about twenty, maybe older, with lovely brown eyes like Jessica. She was rocking back wards and forward, groaning and acting as if she didn't notice them, she had tears in her eyes, and then she began to hum a tune. Suddenly they heard a guard shouting.

"Quiet charlatan," he said. "And make your peace with God, for tomorrow you will hang."

"God will save me!" she shouted. "But not you heathens, you will go to hell."

Jessica and Alicia walked over to her, hoping to help her and then they noticed her chained to the wall. The woman pulled at the chains, as they approached, she seemed frightened, trying to get away from them.

"Please don't be scared," Alicia said. "We want to help you."

"You don't, you want to kill me!" She raged. "You and all your kind!"

"Our kind?" Jessica asked puzzled.

"Yes, charlatans, all of you," she said. "False witnesses, evil prophets, wolves in sheep's clothing."

"I do assure you, we are not charlatans," Jessica insisted.

"What is your name?" Alicia asked.

At that moment the guard came in with her food, the witches made themselves invisible, and observed his state of dress, as he passed them.

"Talking to your familiars, witch?" he said. "Here is you food, enjoy it" and then he left the room.

The witches re-appeared, shocked at the food that she was given, and the way that she was treated.

"Chefs special I see," Jessica said. "Soup of the day and moldy bread with water."

"We can do better than that, can't we Jess!" Alicia said.

"Of course, we are no charlatans" Jessica said using her wand to produce a roast beef meal.

Alicia produced a jug of fresh juice and fresh fruit; everything was presented on plates. The woman was amazing, but apprehensive at first, until she tasted it, experiencing the taste, and then ate most of it.

"My name is Ruby," she said.

"I am Alicia and this is my sister Jessica," Alicia said. "We really are witches."

"Why didn't the guards see you?" Ruby asked.

"We can make ourselves invisibly," Alicia said.

"That's useful," Ruby said.

"It's awesome," Jessica said.

"Now what about clothes?" Alicia said. "Perhaps a coloured dress."

"Alicia, she needs a wash first," Jessica insisted.

Jessica set up a false screen in front of the bars, in three dimension, so that the guards couldn't see them, while Alicia produced a tub full of warm water, with soap and towels.

Jessica produced make up and Alicia designed a suitable dress. When they had finished, Ruby looked so glamourous, she was like a different woman.

Meanwhile, Maya arranged for the ship, to follow the location of Gilbert, in another time zone. He was found in a desert, miles from anywhere, walking along in the baking heat, lost in time. He was thirsty and dehydrated, with cracked lips, just wearing his shirt and trousers rolled up to his knees, looking very anxious. He was so relieved when they rescued him, he had a shower and cream on his sun burnt face.

"Gilbert, your safe now," Maya said. "We will get you home."

"Thank you," he said gratefully.

After this they picked up other poor victims of the box, from various periods of time, each one was shocked, and bewildered by their experience. They were each taken back home, to their planets, and time periods, safe and sound, to their relief. Janet was so grateful to see Gilbert, he looked so well, just a little sun burnt from the desert. As for the box or cabinet, it was burnt down in a field, along with anything else belonging to Branzino and Maria the charlatans.

Jessica and Alicia were conversing with Ruby, trying to find out where she was from, but it was confusing as she couldn't remember everything. At that time, they had taken the three-dimensional screen away, the guards entered the prison cell to take the girl away for execution. The one guard grabbed her chains, while the other one grabbed her by the arms, but they were shocked at the way she looked, both looking at each other.

"What's going on?" one of them said.

"This is sorcery," the other said. "Definitely witchcraft!"
At that moment, the witches appeared, "Leave her!" Jessica said in a deep voice.

They let her go and went to strike Jessica and Alicia with their swords, Alicia produced a sword and attacked one of them, while Jessica uses her powers against the other guard sending him off the ground and against the wall. Alicia used her fencing skills against the one guard, Jessica continues to use her powers by sending the guard up in the air, suspending him for a while, and then dropping him swiftly on the ground. At this point, Maya enters the room, she is surprised to see the guards in trouble.

"Girls, we have to go," she said.

"We are not done yet!" Alicia said.

"Come on, Alicia." Maya insisted.

"Let me fight," Alicia said. "I am not finished with him!"
Maya struck the guard with a lightning bolt. "You are now," she said.

Luna did the same with the other guard, and he fell to the ground, injured.

"Now let's go!" Maya said. "Quickly, before more guards come!"

When they arrived back at the ship, Maya was annoyed about Alicia and Jessica travelling in the box, taking risks.

"Whatever were you thinking?" Maya said. "Risking your lives like that."

"We saved that woman, Ruby!" Alicia said in her defence.

"She did do that, Maya." Luna said in her defence.

"It's not the point Alicia, you are so reckless at times." Maya pointed out.

"I didn't want to do it," Jessica said. "But it is true, we helped that woman."

"She would have been hung!" Alicia stressed.

"You two could have been hung with her," Maya said. "But I acknowledge that you saved her and dressed her nicely from what I can see."

"She looks beautiful," Luna said. "Well done!"

"Where is she from?" Maya asked.

"We don't know," Alicia replied. "She wasn't clear on that."

"Evidence shows that she is from Franmania," Foster said.

Ruby was staring at Strania and Shimick, like they were odd creatures, they were talking to her but she was just staring. It didn't seem right, and so Maya took her to one side, and spoke to her, wanting to know why she was doing this.

"I am sorry, I have never seen green people before," she admitted.

"But, according to the time you were put in the box it was 2506, Foster has just confirmed that you are from the planet Franmania, a peaceable planet near Grancarna, the green planet."

"I don't remember," Ruby replied.

"Then let's go there," Maya said. "You do know that, the charlatans come from there."

"Antonio Branzino and his Sister Maria Branzino, from the planet Franmania, known for fraud, theft and being charlatans through the galaxy, time fugitives," Foster said. "They started out by helping people escape, from space prisons on planets and spacecrafts, cleverly by making them disappear in cabinets. But what they didn't realise were these containers were unpredictable, the controls were unstable and they really did disappear, to various places in time and space," Foster explained.

"It is not surprising that you don't remember, Ruby," Maya said. "Or should I say Galistra, green witch from Grancarna, the green planet."

"That's impossible," Alicia said. "She isn't green?"

"When the original time witches landed on Grancarna, they were affected by the green atmosphere, mainly Shanice and Elaina. Maya explained So, Crystal created an antidote that changed them back, even the shape of their ears and hair colour were affected."

"You have taken this drug to change your body, but it won't last, you will change back," Jessica said.

"Are you taking me back?" Ruby asked.

"We have no choice," Alicia said. "We have to uphold the galactic laws."

"What if I told you where Branzino is," Ruby said. "I know where he is."

"That would help, and we can put in a word for you, on Grancarna," Maya offered.

"I will give you his co-ordinates," Ruby said.

They set course for Franmania, hoping to capture the charlatans, who were sat in their home counting their money and silver trophies. The time witches arrived to catch them putting them in handcuffs, Branzino the slimy fish was unable to riddle off the hook.

He appeared bewildered, as if it wasn't supposed to happen this way, caught at last by his own tricks. Maria just accepted it, knowing her time was up, all that time tricking people, was it worth their future in space prison. As for Ruby or Galistra, they returned her to Grancarna, to face trial, on the way, she changed back into her real self. Not as attractive, as a green witch with a longer nose, pointed ears and a green pigment. Compared to Strania who was also green, but very attractive, and her personality shone through. It became clear to them, why she was staring and seem to dislike them, being one of the green witches. Of course, she could have been ashamed of her past, regretting what she had done on the green planet, after all the green witches were like their dark witch ancestors cruel, scheming and pure evil.

They arrived on Franmania, Ruby was true to her to her word, as she led them to the home of Branzino. They landed close to the area, the plan was to take Ruby to the front door with Maya and Luna, while Alicia and Jessica went around the house to the back door. The front door was open, so they entered consciously Maria was caught, but Branzino tried to escape through the back door. Alicia and Jessica captured him using their magic skills, by shooting lightning out of their wands.

"What do you propose doing to us?" Maria asked.

"You will be taken to space federation headquarters," Alicia replied.

"For what crimes?" Branzino asked.

"Try fraud and endangering lives," Jessica replied. "With your vanishing cabinet."

"Let us return to the ship," Maya said.

The next stop was space federation headquarters, to drop off the criminals,

And then take Ruby to Grancarna. But as they took Branzino and Maria, Ruby tried to escape, she sent the time witches in the air with telekinesis, and ran. A guard fired his laser and knocked her to the ground, after which she was arrested, and kept at headquarters.

The commander sent for the time witches, and said that they might

be needed for more urgent matters, and to wait for instructions.

TOTAL DESTRUCTION

It was a dismal day on the planet Cryrotario, it was a planet where nothing lived, no signs of life just the slow passing of time. The surface was like a reddish brown colour, with craters everywhere, and three moons in the sky. But amidst all this was three bases scattered about, these consisted of a science complex run by androids and humans, a weapons factory and a place where disused robots went to be destroyed and melted down in order to make other androids and weapons. During this process, something went badly wrong, an android that had been sent there, caused a lot of damage. The android known as Delta, was supposed to have been turn off, disconnected and no longer operational. But for some reason switched back on, Delta was aware that he was being terminated, and responded defensively, by attacking the facility.. It began with red lights turning on in his eyes and a clicking sound like mechanical activity indicating that Delta five was activated. Delta knew how to reprogram other robots, and used online circuits to set the sequence off, causing a chain reaction. Firstly Victor 1, and then Bishop 4, followed by Mica 5, all dangerous androids. They eventually sent deadly rays, out of their arms and blew up the entire base, all almost everybody inside, but few survived to tell the tale.

Back at the space federation headquarters, a destress call came in from the weapons factory, it was their next target, They had taken what they could, and blew that one up too, leaving no survivors this time, just a blazing few buildings. Film footage of the horrific attack was sent to headquarters, watched by everyone including the time witches.

The words "Total destruction" was repeated over and over again by a robotic voice, followed by a message about the destruction of mankind.

'Mankind verses machine will end, with the total destruction of mankind, there is no way out for man but total annelation. We reign supreme at last; man has caused his own destruction; he must face the consequences of his own actions'. This was the chilling message sent to the space federation headquarters, following the destruction of the first two bases. The next target was the science base on Cryrotario, where scientists and Androids worked side by side, spaceships stolen from the weapons base two, and vehicles from base one, were used to attack base three.

"I had this awful feeling; something was going to happen." The commander said.

"I have been getting images," Luna said. "Flames and explosions, death and destruction."

"Do you still feel it?" Jessica said.

"Yes, it is very intense," Luna replied. It is like, the light of the world has gone out."

"I see it too," Strania agreed. "Deaths everywhere."

"The space federation is at war against androids." The commander said. "This is no lame threat; we must take action now."

"We will travel to Cryrotario, and try to stop them from there," Maya said.

"I will send Angelica, our bionic weapon," the commander offered. "We will defend our headquarters."

The time witches set the coordinates for Cryrotario, ready to face the enemy of androids, a mighty force building in strength, and causing destruction in their wake. They arrived to see explosions, buildings being destroyed by spacecrafts and armored vehicles. When they landed, they entered the building hoping to find survivor's, the federation ships attacked the android ships, and armored vehicles. Fortunately, the time witches knew their way around the base, and searched for the scientists, amidst the smoke and debris. Some of their robots turned on them, after being programed to kill humans. The time witches fought the androids, using all their powers to defeat them, blowing them to pieces.

Maya was attacked by one of the apart with androids, who took her by surprise, grabbing her arms and trying to break her neck. Angelica jumped in and tore the android apart, limb by limb using her bionic strength, to conquer it. Elaina was close by, saying, "We have your back," while striking more androids.

A familiar voice came over the speakers. "Retreat," he said. "We have bigger fish to catch."

"Bula Seraph," Maya said. "So, he was behind the rebellion."

"He escaped from prison," Luna said, "Was in a space prison, in orbit not far from here."

"He was set free to do this," Maya said. "Is the prison still there?"

"No, it was blown up, after he escaped," Luna explained.

"And they are going to attack the federation headquarters next," Alicia said.

"We better go and save the universe," Jessica said. "Or what is left of it?"

The base was stabilized, making it safe for the surviving scientists, fortunately part of the base was intact, the wounded scientists were taken onto ships, in order to get medical support. Therefore, the time witches headed back to headquarters, to rescue the staff from their mechanical enemies, the deadly androids led by Delta 5 and Bula Seraph.

During the flight Elaina caught up with her cousins Alicia and Jessica, sharing stories of their adventures as time witches.

"You ladies have probably seen a lot already," Elaina said.

"You were certainly not kidding, about your adventures," Alicia said.

"It was all real," Elaina said. "Such an amazing adventure with my time witch friends."

"Vampires were very challenging," Alicia said.

"Did you meet Sienna and Catrina?" Elaina asked.

"Yes, Catrina was in a leather suit, she was a slayer," Jessica said. "Cool outfit."

"We also met Joan of Arc," Alicia said. "I taught her to use a sword."

"Like I taught you, Alicia," Elaina said, reminiscing. "I fought pirates with a sword."

"You also met Blackbeard the pirate," Maya said with my cousin Shanice.

"Shanice made quite an impression on Blackbeard," Elaina explained. "He was an amazing man, misunderstood in history books."

"We did meet a green witch, who was disguised as a white earth girl, who called herself Ruby or Galistra if you use her 'witch' name," Alicia explained. "She is at the federation prison."

"Interesting, she was quite a challenge to the Goblins on Grancarna," Elaina commented.

"I bet you must miss, your adventures in time and space," Jessica said.

"Yes, I do, but my life at the federation is good, with Angelica of course," Elaina said. "You must come to our wedding."

"We would love to," Maya said. "Give us the time and place, are the others coming, Crystal, Natasha, and Shanice?"

"Yes, they are like one big happy family," Elaina explained. "From our time witch days."

The androids reached the federation headquarters, they stayed in space for a while orbiting the earth, while they planned their attack. Bula contacted them to find out what the plan was, and how he could assist them.

"Hello my friends, this is Bula Seraph, wizard and friend," he said.

"Bula Seraph, are you ready to destroy this place?" Delta asked.

"Of course," Bula replied. "With my assistant Sinead, we can get this party started."

"Seek out all humans and kill them, and that will be followed by total destruction."

The other robots each repeated total destruction, and then they went silent waiting for orders. Delta sent a message out to his robots, regarding Bula Seraph just to make his intentions known to them.

"I wish to make it known that, Bula Seraph should die, after we have victory along with his assistant Sinead, they must die."

"Understood, total destruction," Victor replied.

"Total destruction," Mica replied.

"Bula Seraph to die," Bishop agreed.

The ships made their approach towards the planet, they were ready to attack the federation, some of the robots had turned on the federation troops. It was a matter of time before, Delta five gave the orders to attack, preparing the weapons for total destruction.

"Attack!" came the orders from Delta. "Total destruction!"

The ships travelled into the area of the base, blasting buildings in their sights, there were explosions everywhere, some building flattened. At this time, the robots descended on the base wearing parachutes, entering the building by blasting off the doors. Many soldiers lost their lives defending the federation, the androids seemed invincible.

The time witches were on their way, piloted by Luna, who getting disturbed by images of the attack, Strania could also feel it and visualize the devastation. Precognition isn't always a good ability to possess, seeing events taking place in the present or future. A gift or power can be adventitious or a cause for concern, depending on the impact that it has on your life. The main thing is that you are in control, and that it does not control you. One example is Bula Seraph, who allows his powers to control him, and being an entity of the evil wizard Merek, he has no choice but to act evil himself. He has his life mapped out as a carbon copy of Merek, and his madness, seeing destruction as the only means of survival. He has no conscience, or reasoning, no sense of life worth, and without human feeling. The androids are programmed to react as they do, acting out instructions, mechanical versions of Bula in some cases, responding to set instructions.

The battle continued, Delta had penetrated the base with his army, attacking the federation army, by this time help had arrived, attacking the android ships. The battle was underway in space as well as the base, with many casualties. Delta directed Victor and Mica to different corridors, to make sure everyone would be killed. The time witches landed close to the base, they each entered one by one, Alicia and Jessica went into the air vents, and crawled across towards the commanders office. It was a tight squeeze, but a safe way to get there, pushing their way through the narrow metal tunnels. They were getting close to the office, when they heard a noise, like an explosion. They looked through a vent, and saw Victor 1 in the office with the commander, they had to rescue him, he was about to get killed. Alicia took out her wand and poked it through the grid, without thinking she shouted out a spell, "Obliterate!" and the android exploded.

Unfortunately, there were more androids, who responded to her attack, by firing up at them.

"Oh, good thinking, Alicia," Jessica said. "Nice one!"

Fortunately, neither got injured, and they managed to fire again at the androids, disabling them with their wands, and then climbing down to join the commander.

"We need to get to the control room," he said.

"No problem," Alicia said.

"You think," Jessica replied. "If we survive this, I think that I will pick a new career, like pet rescue and without my crazy sister."

Angelica ran down the corridor at great speed, coming face to face with Mica, she ploughed into him, like a bull at a gate, sending him over onto the floor. He got back up and fired at her, the laser narrowly missed her head, and burnt the wall. Angelica used her magic powers to strike again, by telekinesis she forced him to fly into the air, and hit a wall. Elaina was caught in the cross fire at this point, as Mica fired again wounding her in the shoulder. Angelica fired back at him, using her wand, sending a lightning bolt towards him, taking his right arm off, he charged over to Elaina, about to kill her when Angelica fired again, blowing up his left leg. He stumbled again, just missing Elaina as he fell, Elaina crawled to reach her wand, off the ground, touching it with her finger tips. But Mica grabbed her by the throat, and began to strangle her, her body was going limp. Angela raced to her rescue again, and aiming her wand at him, and waiting for the right moment, before shooting at him again, this time she took his head off. His head landed next to Elaina, she noticed his lights go out, no longer operational.

Maya and Luna entered the conference room, just in time to defend some of the staff, who were unarmed. The alarms were sounding, making a deafening whirling sound, some people were panicking, seeking an escape root, some falling over and being fired at by androids. Maya and Luna started to attack them, joined by familiar faces, Natasha, Doran and Crystal, who were also fighting. Flashes of lightning, laser fire and small explosions were all about, the whole area was a war zone.

The commander arrived in the control room, with Alicia and Jessica, they checked the monitors, and noticed that most of the base, was occupied by androids. Everybody fought hard to stop them, reducing their numbers, gradually, trying to immobilize them. The commander arranged for his staff to seal off certain areas of the base, limiting the androids to where they could go. While Alicia and Jessica engaged in battle, defeating androids with their powers, keeping them away from the control room. The battle lasted hours, with many casualties, nobody had chance to rest, they knew once they weakened the androids would kill them all without mercy. Bula remained in his ship, waiting for the android victory, he felt confident that they would win, and then he would travel down to the base and celebrate.

Sinead found out that Crystal was in the base, so she went inside to kill her, she wanted to avenge her mother Davina's death. She searched the corridors, avoiding the conflicts, until she finally saw her fighting a android, she watched for a while and then saw her opportunity to get her. Seizing the moment, she pulled her wand from her clothing, aimed and then sent a bolt of lightning towards her. Crystal was hit in the chest and fell to the ground, no sooner had she struck Crystal, she started to run down the corridor.

She managed to reach the hanger, ready to make her escape, but there was an obstacle in her way. Maya stood in front of her, looking very angry and upset.

"How dare you attack Crystal!" Maya shouted. "Holding her wand out."

"You would dare kill me," Sinead said. "You are a white witch!"

"Try me bitch!" Maya said. "I will take your head off!"

"Crystal killed my mother," Sinead explained. "She deserved to die!"

"One of your own killed your mother, when your mother transformed into Crystal," Maya explained.

"You're a liar!" Sinead insisted.

"It is true," Ruby interrupted. "I have heard this story before."

"Ruby!" Maya said in surprise.

Ruby had fully transformed back to herself by now, a green witch, she was holding a wand towards Sinead.

"You are a green witch, a decedent of the dark witches, why do you take her side?" Sinead asked.

"I am on no one's side," Ruby said. "Just mine."

"Then, you won't object to me killing her," Sinead said aiming her wand.

"Stop!" Ruby insisted. "No one else need die."

Sinead lowered her wand and so did Maya, but just then Sinead appeared to turn her back on them, but suddenly turned back, and sent a lightning bolt towards Maya. Ruby jumped in the way and she was struck in the chest, Maya fired back and hit Sinead in the head.

Ruby lay injured, and Sinead was dead, Maya knelt down beside Ruby, and listened to her speak, Luna appeared beside them.

"Maya, see that I am remembered for doing good," Ruby said. "Take my body back to Grancarna, let me rest there."

"Ruby, we can help you," Maya said.

"No, I am dying," Ruby said. "Please promise to grant my request."

"We will, Ruby." Maya agreed.

With that Ruby passed away, and Maya closed her eyes, sweeping the tears from her eyes.

The battle continued, and the time witches were helping to defeat the android, who had been reduced in numbers, the corridors were clearing with fewer casualties. Most of the android ships had been destroyed, and Gena the time witches ship was in tact. Bula sent a message down to the federation, thinking the androids had been successful.

"Greetings, to those who may be still alive, I expect you to surrender," he said. "I will arrive there in time to celebrate our success, once Sinead has returned, all we want is total destruction of all bases and the annelation of mankind, nice to have met you all. Goodbye time witches see you never!"

Maya replied to his message, with news from the base, and of Sinead which she felt would affect him.

"Bula Seraph, may I just say that, you have failed once again, the androids are few and Sinead has sadly passed away," Maya said. "And now we are after you, you can run, but you can't hide, we will search the ends of the universe for you, and defeat you."

Bula stamped his fist on the table, and shouted, "Damn you, time witches!"

Angelica was still fighting androids, tearing off their limbs, Doctor Adam Grange was reprograming the system and androids, under the supervision of commander John Shepherd. Elaina was in sick bay with Crystal and Alicia, each of them badly wounded, receiving treatment. Delta 5 was making his escape with other androids, pursued by Maya, Luna and Jessica, who were determined to stop them. Two federal ships joined the time witches in the chase, as they flew into space, at remarkable speed. When they finally caught up with them, they had slowed down, turning around to attack the witches. They fired first, narrowly missing Gena, but hitting one of the federation ships. The federation fired back, blowing up one of their ships, they were down to two ships, but continued fighting. Hitting the left side of Gena, causing them to lose some of their engine power, Maya was concerned about getting back, due to the damage. For the next few moments, their was firing from all ships, until another of the android ships was destroyed. Finally, a lucky shot by the time witches, as Jessica fired the weapon a few times, until she blew up the ship with Delta in it.

"Awesome!" she shouted. "Total destruction."

When they returned to federation headquarters, they left Gena in the hanger, she definitely was in need of repairs. So, they all stayed for a few days. It enabled the time witches to catch up, talking to Natasha, Doran and Angelica, and visiting the others in hospital. Elaina had burns on her back and shoulders, Alicia had a broken arm and burns, and Crystal had chest burns and a broken leg.

Zenith, Crystals father was taking care of their daughters Bethany and Natalie, on Aspera, while Natasha and Doran were helping tidy up headquarters. Maya explained Ruby's promise to take her back to Grancarna, and bury her near the mountains, in order for her soul to rest there.

Everybody agreed under the circumstances, that because of her help, and saving Maya's life, she should be considered a white witch and be treated accordingly. It took a while for Crystal to recover, but she eventually went home, with Natasha, Elaina stayed at the space federation headquarters with Angelica, and the time witches went on further adventures, despite Jessica threatening to leave them. In fact Jessica was one of the most dedicated of all of them, and despite her saying such mean things about Alicia, she loved her sister. The Faber sisters were always popular in school, but Alicia was always the out going reckless one, always taking risks. Maya was always the leader amongst the girls, and Luna followed Maya, like a long-lost sister, all together these are the time witches.

TIME

witches

OTHER BOOKS ON SALE

A PARANORMAL EXPERIENCE

by Stephen Sutton

A lot of my work as a writer/author is based on my paranormal activity, hearing, seeing and feeling spirits from infancy. My first experience was when I lived with my grandparents from birth until I reached 4 years old, I was informed by my mother about an incident at that house. I remember some strange events but not this one as I was a mere ten months old, before I was able to walk. She went to check on me in my cot/crib and watched me rise up from a lying position to standing without holding anything. She remembers the room being cold, and put me back down as if I had never risen. After this incident I was constantly haunted by an old lady, who I called a witch, she had been the one who lifted me up that night. I often asked my father to throw her down the stairs, but they never saw her, only me, even my older brother could not see her. This was disturbing, when my parents related the story later in my life.

SARAH'S GHOST

It was in the September of 2012 that I decided to visit my friends in Sweden for a well-earned holiday. I stayed in their new home in a village called Veberöd situated in the South of Sweden near Lund, it was an old Viking village steep in history.

I stayed one of their children's rooms which he had as a temporary room while his father was converting another room into his new bedroom. I had known my Swedish friends for many years and they had spent time with me in England as much as I had spent time with them in Sweden. But this was the first time that I had stayed in this home since 2008 and I was in a different room then.

I had been there a few nights and had tried to think of ideas for a new story called 'cracked porcelain' I was suffering from writer's block and became very frustrated. I took trips out around the village trying to think of things to write, I had done my research and collected characters together, I had also brainstormed ideas onto paper but that's as far as I had got.

Then one night I was awoken by the urge to use the bathroom, I looked at my clock it was two o'clock in the morning, I regretted drinking so late but being a sociable person, I had to have the odd glass of wine while chatting to my friends. I tried to move my legs when suddenly out of the darkness came a light it seemed small at first and then became larger like a crystal ball with something in the middle, it seemed to float in the centre of the room. I went cold and froze in the bed it seemed to emit energy like an electric charge, I felt as if I was being pulled apart and sapped of strength, I began to feel depressed as if my life was ending sinking deeper and deeper into the bed with no way of shouting for help. I was overwhelmed by sadness and felt tears drifting from my eyes and down my cheeks. Then as quick as it began it stopped and vanished, leaving me alone and bewildered, I felt as if I were tied down and gagged like a hostage in an abandoned house. Then I saw another light much like the first one but this time I felt calm and at peace as if this one had restored my energy and breathed fresh life into me. I sighed with relief as it too disappeared and I was able to move my body freely, my arms and legs were fine and I looked back at the time it was three thirty in the morning. I proceeded to go to the bathroom as I walked, I felt as if I were floating on a cloud. This was a truly amazing experience which I share with those who will understand, I thought I was going mad at the time, was this a ghost, an orb or what?

The next morning, I decided not to relate my experience to my Swedish friends and remained in the house, I began to write my story 'Cracked porcelain' my thoughts began to flow and I began to write things down, I wrote fictitious story about a psychiatric nurse called Ruth Ashley. But while I was writing I kept writing the name Sarah over and over again. I had almost outlined the entire book and wrote quite a few chapters, I amazed myself as I had never done this before. Oddly enough I felt something cold over my right shoulder like someone leaning over me and breathing down my ear, then a sensation like hair brushing past my cheek.

I felt compelled to tell someone and waited until my friends were home and watched one of them lighting candles and acting strange, it was as if they knew what I was about to say before I even mentioned it.

"I suppose you think we are odd lighting candles around the room like this?"

"I was a little curious by your actions."

"Well, a while ago we encountered strange goings on in the house, things went missing and found in odd places, lights went on and off randomly and drills and other appliances turned on. One spoke.

"It was so bad that we sought help from spiritualists and the church," said another.

"It would seem that we were haunted by a couple who were evil ghosts, but they eventually went and thought sent away by a friendly ghost called Sarah," they told me.

I was astonished by the things they were telling me and spoke about Sarah visiting me, I mentioned about writing down her name over and over again, the story writing and feeling her presence. They said that they wanted me to experience it before they mentioned it so that I would find out about Sarah for myself.

Sarah remained with me and does so to this day, she tries to communicate with me but often it is when I am writing sometimes, I miss interpret what she is saying for instance she inspired me to write about a patient in cracked porcelain who was suffering from multiple personality syndrome or disassociated identity deficit (DID) But Sarah was trying to explain that she had been reincarnated at least three times as a child, man and woman. She also conveyed that I should help charitable causes and not use all the royalties from books for myself. Sarah is a charitable person and does not believe in capitalist views.

Sarah has helped me with many stories to date and will only visit me when she thinks I need help much like a guardian angel, she felt that I needed help and she was also able to convey her thoughts through me. I visited a medium and she saw Sarah standing over my right shoulder, she described Sarah as slim and beautiful with hazel eyes and long flowing hair. I am sure that I have drawn a picture of her which I keep in my bedroom so that I can imagine her while I am writing stories.

I cherish the thought that Sarah inspires me to write and hope that one day she will appear before me like the orb and speaks to me about herself and the life or lives she led in the past.

THE SPIRITS OF GROUND ZERO

It was in the year 2012 that I visited New York city; I was in Sweden the year before having encountered a ghost called Sarah amongst other strange events. Sarah had helped me to write a novel called 'Cracked porcelain', which is now on sale on Amazon with my other books.

During my stay in Manhattan, I encountered other strange experiences which led to writing another book. I travelled around Manhattan originally on a tour bus in order to orientate myself around the city. I had no idea at this point that I would be experiencing ghostly apparitions in and around ground zero, the memorial garden where the world trade centre twin towers had once stood. I made plans to visit various places and booked to9 go to ground zero, I was excited to visit there because I wanted to pay my respects to those who died during the 9/11 disaster when the terrorist planes crashed into the twin towers.

Needless to say, I was astounded by what I saw, but prepared for what was about to happen as I ventured into ground zero, the foundation of both the twin towers remained and had been transformed in to two square fountains with plaques around the outer walls that had the names of the victims printed on them. As I read the names I was overwhelmed with sorrow and shed a tear for those lost, I suddenly went cold at this point and the area seemed eerie as if I was not alone. Of course, other visitors were there but they felt distant and I felt something brush past me, I turned around but no one was close to me, then I swear that I saw the faint outlines of people walking through the fountains and past visitors as if they didn't exist. The figures seemed like lost souls left behind to tell the tale of how they died, I heard thuds as if heavy sacks were being dropped around me, I realised that I was standing beneath the place where the south tower had stood and that the sound was like the bodies of jumpers falling from the tower to their fate. It was that or burning to death in the tower but either was no way to die.

I felt a pulling sensation on my t shirt and turned around, but again no one was there, I felt an overwhelming sadness as I once again turned to read the plaques. I felt a pulling again this time it was stronger and I was being led to the memorial building where a computer was fixed into the wall and a keyboard below. I was astonished to see an image on the screen of a man who had died and I read all about him, the most amazing thing was that I had been pulled away from his plaque and was now seeing his photograph as if he was trying to converse with me. I can't reveal his name or others as it would not be proper and out of respect for them, but I was enlightened and did begin to understand what had happened. I wrote notes on these events and waited until I got home before I actually compiled my story based on the 9/11 called 'For the love of Charlotte' I wrote about what I experienced initially but then researched the actual events from eye witnesses although my information came from ghosts and then I formed my characters from these people and others to make a love story with Charlotte from Manchester England and Harry from New York who met in Rome and fell in love, eventually Charlotte joined Harry in New York and events led to the 11th September 2001 which was of course when the twin towers were hit by terrorist planes.

It was a difficult story to write and I had problems thinking up a suitable end, which I obviously cannot reveal, but those who have read it were surprised and shocked. Unfortunately, I self-publish my work and so I have not reached a wide audience and so I use the internet for advertising, some people slated me for writing this story and accused me of profiting out of someone else's misery, however I did not do this for that reason, I wanted to let people know that I care and how sad I was at hearing of such a horrid thing to happen to fellow humans. I love the Americans and want some of my royalties to go to charity such as ground zero and those victims' families also to the brave rescuers. Many people were affected by the disaster and I hope that my book 'For the love of Charlotte' comforts them and shows how we feel about a tragedy such as this. My cousin Paige agreed to model for the front cover of the book as Charlotte as she too believed in helping raise money for ground zero and remember those brave people from the 9/11.

PADDED CELL by Stephen Robert Sutton

Listen to me scream

Listen to me shout

I am letting you know

That I am still about

Hitting all the walls

Swearing all the time

Bruising all my body

Isn't it a crime

I never knew what happened to me

I try to rationalise

Is it because I am mad

In this odd disguise

The madness is in my mind

Its started getting to me

Please get me out this padded cell

Come on set me free

THE GHOST by Stephen Robert Sutton

I speak to you

About the ghost

To explain it all

It's about a host

A man that carries

A deadly thing

A nasty virus

Or plague like thing

He makes his journey

Far and wide

With this deadly virus

Deep inside

He touches those

Who stands so close

This evil man

Who is called the ghost?

People die

A painful death

With burns and boils

And lack of breath

No one see him

Travelling near and far

But just leave them

With his deadly scar

The ghost could be

Standing by your side

You cannot escape him

You cannot hide

NOBODY LISTENS by Stephen Robert Sutton

Nobody listens

Nobody cares

Nobody wants to

Nobody dares

Frightened to speak

Left on the shelf

No one understands

My mental health

Vicious and spiteful

Echoes remain

No one is listening

To those insane

I speak of my illness

My problems in life

You cannot see madness

Not without strife

The darkness is present

The demons appear

You cannot see them

But believe me they're here

Nobody listens

To the words that I say

They think I am sane

But I muddle through the day

One day they will listen

And remember my name

Find my poor body

And say what a shame

Nobody listens

Nobody cares

Nobody wants to

Nobody dares

PORTRAIT OF MY SOUL by Stephen Robert Sutton

Paint a picture

On canvas for me

Using colours

That plainly I see

Dark colours of

Purple and grey

Depicting my mood

At the end of the day

Paint it in detail

Like a good photograph

Don't make it funny

Don't make me laugh

Make it so dull

But clear enough to see

Paint me a portrait

Do this for me

You are painting my soul

This looks very real

Paint me a conscience

So, I can feel

Deep in my thoughts

I remember my pain

Scrub it all out

And start it again

MIRACLE

One fine summers day in central park, a blind girl enters the park through the east gates. She walks cautiously along the edge of the pathway, and reaches a line of benches, sitting on the centre bench. She is an attractive girl in her early twenties, with long dark hair and large brown eyes, dressed in a white blouse and a patterned skirt. She is wearing socks and trainers, and using a white stick in which to guide her on her way. She is able to see, dark figures and shapes, apart from this she is blind. She has only recently found the courage to go out alone, and liked this particular part of the park, because it was a little busy, and yet fairly quiet, so that she can hear, birds and other creatures of nature. Sometimes people would join her on the bench, and have a conversation, just a general chat about the weather or other things. On this particular day, a man joined her, he was a slim man with short dark hair and a beard, a man in his thirties.

"Excuse me," he said politely. "Is anyone sitting here?" he asked.

"I don't think so," she replied. "I am blind, so I can't say for sure."

"Oh, my goodness, sorry," he said awkwardly.

"It's okay," she said. "Easy mistake to make."

"How long have you been blind?" he asked.

"From childhood as far as I remember," she said. "My name is Alison."

"I am Michael," he replied. "Do you mind me eating my sandwiches here?"

"Not at all," Alison said.

Michael opened his sandwich box, and began to eat as quietly as he could, so that he didn't annoy Alison.

"Ham and tomato," she said. "I can smell it."

"Is it offensive?" he asked.

"No, it smells nice," she said. "It's making me hungry."

"Would you like some?" he offered.

"No thanks," she replied. "I am meeting my family for lunch."

"Another time maybe," Michael said, removing a flask from his bag.

"Coffee," she said. "That smells strong."

"Yes, I would offer you some but I only have one cup," he said sipping it.

"I am fine," she said. "Another time maybe."

"Any time," he agreed.

"My other senses compensate for my blindness," she explained. "Such as hearing, smell and taste."

"You are a very brave girl," he said. "I bet your family are proud of you."

"I am used to it by now," she said. "I try to be as independent as possible, so that I am not a burden to anyone."

"But, wouldn't you like to see?" he asked curiously.

"Yes, but that is never going to happen," she replied. "Not according to the hospital."

"I am sorry to hear that," he said.

"Like I said I live with It." she commented.

Michael left the bench, telling Alison that he would be back tomorrow, at the same time, in case she wanted to meet him again. Alison said that she would be there, she was curious about this man, who obviously showed an interest in her. She had gone to meet her family in a café and had lunch, she explained about meeting Michael, and they advised her to take care, talking to strangers.

The following day, Alison went to the same bench, at the same time, and sat waiting for Michael. He came along a short while afterwards, and saying hello he sat beside her.

"Hi Michael," she said cheerfully.

"Are you well?" he asked.

"Yes, I am," she replied. "How are you?"

"Good thank you," he said, opening his sandwich box. "I took the liberty of making you sandwiches."

"That is very kind of you," she replied. "What have you made?"

"Smell them," he offered.

"Beef and tomato," she said sniffing. "My favourite."

"I brought a spare cup too," he said, bringing out his flask. "A picnic," Alison joked.

"Are you religious, do you believe in God?" he asked.

"Are you serious?" she replied. "Me, believe in god."

"I am sorry, I didn't mean to offend you," he said.

"I blame God, because I am like this," she replied. "Just as a crippled person or any other disability."

"People often blame God," he said. "When something bad happens, but is God to blame?"

"No offence but God hasn't helped," she said bitterly.

"Have you ever prayed or put faith in God?" he asked.

"I have prayed in the past," she admitted.

"Maybe he has heard you," Michael said.

"Well, I am still blind," she said bitterly. "So, no answer there."

"One day you will see the light," he said confidently.

Michael said goodbye and offered to see her tomorrow; Alison offered to make the sandwiches for their next meeting.

The next day, they met again, this time Michael arrived first and he was sitting waiting for Alison. He watched her enter the gate and approach him at the bench, being careful not to trip over him, and then sat down beside him.

"Hi Michael you are early," she said.

"Eager to get away from the busy streets," he said.

"How have you been?" she asked.

"Good, how about you?" he asked back.

"I was thinking about what you said about God," she explained. "About having faith."

"Yes, was I going on?" he asked.

"No, what you said made sense," she replied. "About the bible and Miracles."

"Jesus cured many people including the blind," Michael explained. "The great healer."

"What do you look like, can I feel your face?" she asked.

"Yes, of course," he said, turning towards her.

She felt around his face, running her fingers through his beard, touching his hair and around his eyes and forehead.

"You are a handsome man," she remarked. "Wise and kind."

"Thank you," Michael said.

Their meeting ended for the day and they both went their separate ways as usual. They met the next day, and as usual shared their lunch. They had met Monday to Friday and each day took it in turns making a little picnic to share. Week two consisted of the same things and week three too, in fact they ventured into other foods and a nice café.

But mainly in the park, where it was nice and quiet, a place of peace and solitude, suitable for talking and listening.

Alison was curious, about the miracles that Jesus had performed, such as healing the lame, the lepers and of course the blind. She was interested to hear how and why he did this, what was his purpose on earth and why did he sacrifice himself for mankind. "Jesus was the son of god," Michael explained. "He demonstrated in his miracles, just what was possible, in order to help mankind who had faith in him."

"Do you believe this?" Alison asked.

"I believe he was sincere," Michael replied. "He felt compassion for the vulnerable people and demonstrated his love by curing them. They had faith in him and he let them see the light, their faith had set them free, and they became his followers."

"Can you demonstrate how he did this?" she asked.

"Yes, if you wish, I will do this," he offered. "Just open your mind to God and have faith in him."

"Okay," she agreed. "I trust you."

"Sit and face me," he instructed. "Close your eyes, I am going to touch your eye lids with my thumbs, I will gently rub them. Listen to my words, as I do this, open your heart to God, let him see you as you are, your kindness and sincerity."

Michael began rubbing her eyes gently, she felt a breeze and what felt like a light spray of water like raindrops dripping onto her face, she felt a tingle down her spine and a bright light shining onto her face. Michael was praying while he rubbed her eyes, she listened carefully to his words, and almost drifted off to sleep, feeling totally relaxed. After this, he told her to open her eyes, she did so, but was disappointed when she found that she still could not see.

"How do you feel?" he asked her.

"Exhilarated, but I still can't see," she replied.

"Have faith, continue to believe and you will see the light," he assured her.

They left the park and went their separate ways, when she returned home her mother was their making something to eat, she could see that Alison looked upset.

"What's wrong Alison?" she asked. "Can I help?"

"No one can," she replied. "Not even God."

"Have you been talking to that man again?" her mother asked.

"Yes, but he is so kind and understanding," Alison said with tears in her eyes. "He is different from anyone I have ever met, but very religious."

"Don't be upset, but your father and myself have seen you in the park, but never seen him," she said curiously.

"He was there," Alison said. "I haven't made it up."

"I believe you," she said, hugging Alison.

Alison went to bed early after her meal, and thought about her day with Michael, trying to understand what had happened. It was at this time she felt something on her eye lids, rubbing them like Michaels thumbs, with a tingling throughout her body. She thought about his words in prayer, that repeated over and over again in her head.

"Father, hear my prayer, comfort this child of yours, feel her love and devotion, feel compassion and restore her sight, let her see the light, Amen."

She fell asleep, dreaming of this man, and his kindness, imagining him as a special man, Godly and full of kindness, helping the vulnerable and weak. Just like Jesus of Nazareth, who died to save mankind, by sacrificing himself for the sins of many, this was her enlightenment.

"The next morning, she awoke into a new world, she could see the sunlight appearing through a crack in the curtains, things were blurred but she could see. Her new world was the world of sight, a brand-new place for her, with an array of colours all around her. She was so excited, she called out to her mother and father, asking them to come to her.

"Mother, please come here," she shouted. "Dad come here."

They rushed into the room fearing the worst, she was so excited and began jumping on the bed, and looking around at different objects.

"What is it, Alison?" her mother asked. "What's wrong?"

"I can see," Alison said. "I can really see."

"That's impossible, you know what your doctor said." Her father said.

"You would never see," her mother explained. "What nonsense has this man put in your head?"

"I can see the curtains, that teddy and your faces" she said describing everything in sight, but she couldn't explain colour as she had never seen it before.

Her parents were astonished, hugging and kissing her, appearing so happy, but confused.

"How did this happen?"

"It had to be Michael; it was a miracle," Alison insisted.

"There is no such thing as miracles," her father said.

"Stan, you don't know that," her mother said.

"Martha, there is no such thing, we need to take her to the doctors," Stan advised.

"I know," Martha agreed. "Get her tested."

"Will you teach me colours?" Alison asked. "I must see Michael, thank him for my sight."

Alison got ready to go out, she had a shower, and chose her clothes from the wardrobe, for the first time, everything remained blurred. But she ventured out taking her white stick, that she had used constantly, packing sandwiches in her bag. Her parents were watching her in the distance, hoping to catch sight of Michael, and thank him for restoring her sight. However, he did not appear, much to Alison's disappointment, she stayed for an hour, people spoke to her in passing, but no one had seen him, they only ever saw her on the bench.

Later that day, she went to the doctors, who examined her and to his astonishment, she could see, her sight was now clearer and objects clear. The doctor referred her to the hospital, for a further examination, in the meantime her father taught her colours, and her mother taught her to read and write.

Months passed by and she was getting more confident, she could see clearer with perfect vision, she was able to distinguish colours and read perfectly well. The specialists were amazed at her progress and they were baffled by her being able to see. Although, they didn't believe the story about Michael, thinking it was part of Alison's imagination, and that miracles don't exist. But, when Alison was in the hospital, she heard a voice that she recognised, she entered a side ward and lying in a bed was none other than Michael.

"Michael!" She shouted excitedly. "It's you."

"Alison, you look well," he said.

"I can see," she said. "You cured me."

"Alison, your faith cured you," he explained. "Those who believe will see the light, remember this and do good, help others."

Alison turned as her parents appeared in the room, they seemed puzzled at her behaviour.

"This is Michael," she said introducing him.

"Where is he, Alison?" her father said.

Alison looked back to the bed and it was empty, which confused her.

"He was here, honestly," she said. "I was just talking to him."

"Let's get something to eat," Martha said, leading them to the canteen.

On arrival Alison was still talking about Michael, being a real person, she insisted that she didn't imagine it, he was real, but she could not prove it. Across from her on another table a young girl was listening, and told Alison her story, about the same man who had helped her to walk after being crippled by a road accident.

"Specialists said that I would never walk again, but here I am walking again, thanks to Michael, who gave me faith to do this," she explained.

"I met him in the park, he was sat on a bench eating sandwiches, he offered me one and spoke kindly to me and saw me as a person, often people talk to my carers and not me."

"What did he look like?" Alison asked.

"A man about thirty with a beard, slim his hair was over his ears, nicely dressed," she explained. "I am Judy, nice to meet you."

"I am Alison," she said. "And this is my parents."

"Did anyone else see him?" Martha asked.

"No, people think that I made him up," Judy said. "But he was real, he touched me and cured me, by praying and told me to have faith, he said I would see the light."

"That's incredible," Stan said.

"Yes, and I can name others who have been cured," Judy said. "By the grace of God."

"I wonder why we can't see him," Martha said.

"It maybe because his mission is to help people in need," Judy explained. "He is not an exhibitionist, he does not expect praise, just for us to do good and believe in God."

"He wants us to help others, to do good unselfishly," Alison said.

"I did not walk straight away, it took a few days to get my strength and confidence," Judy said. "But with faith and determination I walked, nobody can explain how or why, it was a miracle."

"Perhaps we can work together in charity work, Judy." Alison suggested.

"I would like this," Alison agreed.

True to their word they did work together in various charities, and became good friends, they also attended church together, and shared their experience with others. They did meet others, who had experienced their own miracles, each meeting Michael and each describing similar things. Over the years, they met more people with similar stories, reassuring them that Michael did exist.

www.ingramcontent.com/pod-product-compliance
Lightning Source LLC
Chambersburg PA
CBHW070527310726

48976CB00002BA/564